I0618498

Spell Bound

By Kenneth Niles

Kendu Press
KenduPress@icloud.com
2017

Spell Bound
Copyright © 2017 Kenneth Niles

Dedicated to my loving wife, Ethel Pacheco Niles, and my loving sister, Mary Ellen Niles Howard, of Florence, MA.

To Ethel, for her wholehearted encouragement and patience, always wanting only the best outcomes for me.

To Mary Ellen, a big supporter of this work; her abiding faith and friendship saw me though some of my darkest moments, and helped me ultimately prevail over many of my inner demons.

Acknowledgements:

A special thanks to James Quinn, of Northampton, MA, whose wholehearted encouragement and invaluable editing, throughout the writing process, made this book a real possibility.

A special thanks to Ms. Mia Cortez, of Kensington, MD, for her editing services and her professional guidance, helping me to develop my creative abilities and to greatly improve the overall nature of the manuscript.

CONTENTS

TO THE LETTER: AN I FOR AN I

It was the start of the day shift when the first patient arrived.

"What do we have, Bernese?"

"Kyle Wilson. Auto accident," said the nurse at his side. She didn't seem fazed.

The doors swung open, and another victim was rolled in, blood oozing from his mouth and leg.

Dr. Richard Angle looked up briefly before turning back to his new patient. "Kyle, can you hear me?" he asked, lifting his eyelids to probe with his light.

"Non-responsive," he muttered to himself. "Looks like another TBI."

An instrument tray clattered to the floor as another gurney rolled into the room.

"Get this one up to the OR, *stat*, heavy abdominal hemorrhage," an attendant said, as the gurney was hurriedly pushed back out of the room.

"Right out of the gate and we're off to a flying start," Dr. Angle said, and then, continuing with Kyle, "Bernese, go ahead, hang 1 mg IV propranolol, every six hours. I'll reassess at the end of shift, and send a note to Dr. Norris for an eval of another coma case, when he has time."

Fading in and out of his senses, Kyle picked up on what Dr. Angle said next. Very bright lights and strong antiseptic odors stirred Kyle's senses as he heard the doctor say, "A nice looking young man, where's he from?"

He also picked up on the sting of the needle.

"What the hell is going on," he tried to say, but his lips wouldn't move.

"Jesus, I can't talk," and then he tried moving—nothing! "God, I'm trapped and no one knows."

He thought back. Just that morning he had been due at the library conference in Boston, about two hours from his home in Hanover. He should have known it would be slippery. He had given it a second thought as he scraped the heavy coat of ice off the windshield, cursing himself for having forgotten his gloves.

"I hope the roads are going to be okay," he had thought. Then he remembered the curve, the oncoming car, hitting the brakes, and now, this strange place. "Obviously, the hospital, and those God-awful lights," he thought.

As a supervisor at a University Library in New Hampshire, Kyle had felt duty bound to get to the conference, in spite of the weather, but he could have listened to his folks, who had suggested he stay overnight.

Things had been looking up for Kyle. He was the supervisor of Circulation, Interlibrary Loan and Systems. Now in his mid-40's, he often wondered if everyone struggled like he had to get settled in life. He was still close to his birth family, but he'd finally met someone, although he hadn't taken the plunge of marriage yet.

Interrupting his thought-train, he heard Bernese agreeing with the kind doctor. "I'll bet he's real popular with the ladies."

"You better notify his next of kin," the doctor replied.

"There are several Wilsons in the directory. I'll see what I can do," Bernese replied.

"God, I feel so strange, that stuff she stuck in my arm." Kyle tried to say something more, "What the hell?" His head seemed to be spinning. No one was paying any attention, no matter how hard he tried to speak. He could still hear everything, and he couldn't quiet the questions in his mind. "What the hell is happening?"

Kyle heard a different voice, "My he certainly is odd looking."

"I wonder what he is."

Kyle looked up. He was in a space with blackboards and little desks with small chairs.

"God, this looks like my second-grade classroom." He thought of Ms. Noble teaching cursive on the blackboard, and how he would just gaze out the window and daydream.

"Where am I?" he asked, looking dazed as he took in his surroundings.

"You are in the Land of Letters."

While its voice sounded human, what stepped out of the shadows was far from it.

Standing before him was a being of a rather peculiar shape. It was a letter A, in fact, as odd as that may sound.

"What do you mean?"

"Choose your words carefully, stranger," it warned. "We are not given to waste here."

"Who do you think you're talking to?" Kyle asked angrily.

"There's no need to take that hostile tone," it replied.

Just then another voice piped up. This time, a letter F stepped into the light. "I wonder if he's a new one. It's been so long, you know, since we've had any new additions."

And yet another revealed himself, a letter D. "Oh my, yes! Wouldn't it be delightful, I've grown awfully sick of seeing the same old faces."

The first creature replied, "Of course not! You two should know better. After all these eons, a new addition is out of the question."

This got Kyle's attention and, even though he couldn't open his eyes, he was able to get a good look at the group, which by now had grown in size. It seemed they were all giant letters, but all of them dressed and made up slightly differently, with gossamer clothes in a medley of different colors, some younger and others older—as a group they looked quite collegial. Oh, yes! The very one with whom he'd been conversing strongly resembled an A. "Funny," he thought, "a pretty fuzzy A, with a blond tassel of hair at the top and round, penetrating eyes; God, this is crazy, but he looks strangely like Mr. Moriarty, another grade-school teacher – those bulging eyes." Nostalgia settled over him.

"He was a teacher who knew what kids needed, off to the gym to play games and always friendly, talking to you and not always trying to tell you something."

Then coming closer, the A brought Kyle back, remarking in a baritone voice, "I am the letter A, but you can call me Blondie, like my friends do. Would you care to introduce yourself?"

This all seemed so strange to Kyle, that he was in the midst of a bunch of creatures, apparently different letters of the alphabet. He knew that generally he had always been considered good looking, some even said handsome. Now he found himself feeling out of place and uneasy. "What the hell is going on! Christ, I know I always thought I was different, I guess self-centered, but why this place?" he thought. Still, he responded as he normally would. "I'm Kyle Wilson."

The statement caused a murmuring in the group. "Please do not joke with us. What letter are you?"

"Letter?" Kyle stammered. Dumbfounded at his surroundings, he noticed right next to the A were some B's and C's looking intently on, with other figures close by, but it was strange distinguishing one from the other. One B had pronounced features, the other a streamlined look, while one of the C's looked outlandishly convoluted. As he looked the group over, some were slanted generally to the right, others seemed to stand out more clearly and a larger share of them were smaller in size.

"We're waiting!" Blondie said, shaking Kyle from his reverie.

"I just told you who I am and I don't like being put upon! Where I come from we treat strangers with a little respect," Kyle had found his voice.

"Oh yeah?" Blondie replied, "Well, if you want to stay here, you must tell us who you are."

Just then Kyle heard P say to Q, "He really could pass for an I."

At this, the letter I came through the crowd, with a very angry look about him.

"You two never seem to mind your own business," he bellowed. "Why he looks about as much like an I as an L or a T does. I think he's an imposter."

As Kyle stood up stretching and yawning there came a screech of satisfaction from the I. "There!" he said. "Just as I thought. Now he's trying to look like an X."

At this, curiosity overcame the group and they started closing in on Kyle. He was so overcome with emotion that he sensed he was about to clock Blondie, so, he backed away, and by now almost everywhere he looked there were more of them.

Deciding now on flight, he turned and ran towards a doorway hoping to escape, but two guards stepped forward to block his path.

Each guard was an X, and one of them was talking to him. "You are an imposter. We must not let you pass; you have tried to imitate us. We do not like plagiarists in the Land of Letters."

"Look, what's going on? I haven't done anything! What's more I'm sick of being pushed around. This is no way to treat a stranger!" Kyle blurted out. "And, what's this plagiarism stuff? I thought I was only stretching; I haven't done anything wrong."

The guards did not pay any attention to him, although they seemed to know Kyle was trying to talk to them.

"Get a load of this guy. He really thinks he can just come barging in here like he owns the place," one guard said to the other, while adjusting his tunic; "God, they make these things so tight. I wonder where they get them, anyway." Continuing, he asked, "Are you going to the 'B' tonight?"

"Nah, my nose gets out of joint at every one of these. It isn't like we haven't all been through these games a million times."

Kyle interrupted again.

"Patience, buddy," The guard said.

Kyle was near his boiling point again, but he also noticed that in all the excitement he had been oblivious to the noise of the group that now engulfed him.

The group, now jovial, chatting and laughing amongst themselves, as Blondie addressed him. "It's okay, stranger, or Kyle, rather," he said. "It took us a while, but we finally realize what you are."

"Well, it's about time!" Kyle said as he gathered his composure, breathing a sigh of relief.

"We understand that you are not aware of our etiquette, although you are perhaps more aware of it than you might guess," Blondie said.

"Oh?" Kyle questioned.

"It's really very simple," he replied, "something like I before E, except after C, and that sort of thing."

"Spelling you mean? Why didn't you just say so in the first place," Kyle asked.

"That's right." "We are always addressed in groups. Ah, that is with the two exceptions of myself and the I. For instance, you would never address B without addressing, perhaps E, or maybe U or T, or me, that is A, and D and so forth."

"I've got it, I've got it!" Kyle protested. "Jeez, you guys must think I'm dumber than dumb." Then, with no little amount of mental gymnastics he proceeded to properly introduce himself. Interestingly, his introduction to Y came about with E, A, S and Y, a paradox to be sure; as his second greeting was to B, O, T, H, and E, a tragic insult to each one, until R stepped forward, grasping his hand in greeting and saved the day.

"Spelling," Kyle mused out loud. "It's funny, but I was taught to spell using the sight method. You know, the whole word whole language approach, to reading and learning—so I just wing it most of the time. You guys really put me on the spot, you know!"

"Yeah, we could tell by the miscue when you greeted B, O, T, H, and E. Of course, you could have always taught yourself phonics. But I'd guess you're one of those stubborn ones who won't learn anything unless it's served up to them on a silver platter."

"What do you mean? I've taught myself lots of things," Kyle protested, thinking back to his family who he had often overheard parsing phrases, talking about spelling and pronunciation. But it seemed odd to him that he hadn't caught

7

on. Was this why he was so self-conscious, unsure of himself and, even why he was here now?

"Yeah, sure, but spelling? That's beneath you?"

Blondie went on probing.

"What is it you said you do?"

"I didn't. But I'm a librarian."

A collective gasp reverberated around the room.

"And you actually look things up and find them too?" Blondie asked, this time his tone was dripping with sarcasm.

"Look, I get by!" Kyle angrily replied. "Of course, wouldn't you know it, but here I am without my trusty dictionary. You've really caught me with my pants down, so to speak. I'm confused; I had no idea anything like this ever existed," he exclaimed.

"It's amazing," answered Blondie.

"What's that?" Kyle asked.

"How blind humans are!" Blondie's voice grew in passion and certainty as he went on.

"They see nothing where there is something and something where there is nothing. Don't you see that we, not so unlike your own kind, take on different roles, which are often best effected by many different and colorful garbs," Blondie said, gesturing around to other letters with his right arm, that he normally held across his belly, as part of his normal posture. Why, have you not seen me, and many other distinguished A's, in the finest gold raiment, adorning some of the great literary treasures of your world? Or is it that you are like most of your kind, who toss us to the wind with the likes of nothing on our backs, save a few scars rent in passing? We don't like being mistaken or taken for granted either! Do you not realize how subtle, flexible and beautiful we can be? I know you think you know all about us, being a librarian and all."

With this thought just hanging there, Blondie inquired, "By the way, what brings you here?"

"Well, I don't really know, and while it seems that it should be a natural place for me, I couldn't have imagined it would be anything like this!"

"On the other hand, I can't remember when my family wasn't immersed in letters, words and phrases. I guess with that background you might think I'd be a great speller, but I fell through the cracks. So, I don't really know where I belong right now, but I sure hope I haven't landed in some kind of purgatory or where I'm not wanted, because I don't like being pushed around."

Kyle thought back to when he was trying to learn to read. His family had bought the first-grade textbook for him to help with his reading and coached him at home, but this had also carried the message that he was different. Their intentions were the best, of course, but he didn't pick up on that, only that he needed help was part of every lesson at home. This was a part of his difficulties growing up; he knew what it felt like to feel different.

Kyle's attention shifted back as he heard, "No one's going to push you around!" exclaimed Blondie. "We were just a little confused at first. It isn't every day we get one of your kind who joins us."

"Thank you. I do feel better now, but I sure would like to get back to my regular life." Kyle paused, thinking of those early years and his difficulty with the basics of spelling and grammar. How odd, that at the same time he had a strange way with words.

"Easy does it," said Blondie. "You better try to make the best of it while you're with us. Some of our etiquette might actually rub off. In fact, there's a 'B' tonight and you'd be very welcome to attend. You might pick up a thing or two."

"'B', what do you mean?" Kyle asked.

"Spelling-B," Blondie replied.

"No thanks!" Kyle rushed to reply. "Well, I'm not finding fault or anything, but I'm not really very comfortable with those kinds of games and this place is so stark."

"Stark you say. You just happened on us in the *in-between*, outside the real Land of Letters, just another place outside our regular domain. Look, it's obvious you're distracted, but you better stick around with us for a while. Maybe your perspective will change and you'll hold us in a little higher regard when you leave," Blondie said. "You can't just run away every time you don't like something, you know. So, come-on, let's get going."

Blondie grabbed his hand and to Kyle's surprise, he turned and led him right into the blackboard.

"Looks just like Ms. Noble's," Kyle was so stunned he had to laugh. "And I can even smell the chalk."

Again, he found himself asking, "What is this place?" Like the calm after a storm, the scrambled letters that were swirling around in clouds of chalk dust suddenly settled down into a rather organized scene.

"This is it, the real Land of Letters," Blondie exclaimed, rather proudly. "We live here."

Kyle took a step back. Thin lines resembling streets were lined up below papier-mâché buildings.

"We never know how it looks to the mind's eye. Everyone's imagination is different, of course. It's truly the manifestation of that old saying, *it is what you make of it.*"

Paying no attention to Blondie, Kyle was totally consumed with what he could now plainly see.

"My God, what an array."

Naturally, he could have picked Arial, Bookman, Courier, Helvetica, Lucida, even **Braggadocio**, *Brush Script* and 𝔏𝔲𝔠𝔦𝔡𝔞 𝔅𝔩𝔞𝔠𝔨𝔩𝔢𝔱𝔱𝔢𝔯 out of a line-up. But there were hundreds of others, and they may as well have been in Greek.

There were hundreds of them. Some were bold, others slanted or italic. There was only one thing that seemed to distinguish them. They were either all caps or all lowercase.

Blondie momentarily turned to talk with another letter, but then just disappeared, then reappeared as he turned back.

"Is this a different dimension? Where did you go?" Kyle asked.

Blondie had been smirking, but was now laughing loudly. "Of course not, but it's just two dimensions here. Don't worry, after you're here for a bit you'll find you can easily read between the lines, as it were. When we're facing you it's easy to see us, but when we turn sideways, you'll have to remember who that line you see in our stead really is. Also, we letters, we're kind of clannish. Three-dimensional letters hang out over in the next village, not to mention other villages with characters other than us English-Latin's, like Greek, Cyrillic, Arabic, Hebrew and Chinese to name just a few.

So I guess some of the others were Greek after all, Kyle thought, but he kept it to himself.

Another A, with a dark swarthy complexion and beady little eyes, lost in large arching eyebrows, came up to them.

"Hi, Blondie. So, who's your friend,?" he asked.

"Oh hi, Archie, just another I, Arial type, but he's generally called Kyle." Turning to Kyle, Blondie continued, "Kyle I'd like you to meet another A, a friend I call Archie."

"Well I guess it's true that anything goes these days," Archie, replied, while looking Kyle over.

"No offense, Kyle, it's just small talk," Blondie said, sensing Kyle was getting his hackles up.

"What brings you here, anyway?" Archie asked.

Blondie jumped in with a save, but too late. "He's from the other side… it's a long story."

"I'm perfectly able to speak for myself, if you don't mind," Kyle interrupted, standing up and shaking off some remaining chalk dust. He looked bewildered, but as resolute as always.

"God only knows how I got here. I am starting to think coming here is my penance."

"Please don't think of being here like that. In fact, we hope you'll have a different view of us when you leave. Just look around and you'll see we have our own ways of enjoying existence too," Blondie said.

By this time, Kyle had gotten accustomed to the noise. There was something going on in every corner of this land! Taking it all in was a task in itself.

In the distance, he thought he saw groups of words of different shapes and colors being pulled apart and put together again. Amidst laughter and yelling, dozens of letters appeared to be jumping in basins, like swimming pools.

"What's going on over there?" he asked.

"Oh they're just freshening up before the games." Blondie explained...

"...you know, crosswords, anagrams, puzzles and the like."

"And that smell, is it… Ink?" Kyle asked.

"Our lifeblood! We live and die by ink." Blondie replied.

Just then some other colorfully encircled objects came out of the pools and went running by.

"What are those?" Kyle asked.

Both A's started laughing, as Blondie explained, "Those are called emoji, and they're relatively new to our world. Word is that they are just using our facilities until they get their own village."

At an area, right in front of them, Kyle could see letters forming different lines and as he looked closely, he read, C H I L D H O O D; then looking to the next line, A N X I E T Y came into his view. "Holy cow! What is this, are you guys trying to tell me something?"

"I told you, we never know how the Land of Letters looks to the mind's eye. Everyone's imagination is different, and it's really what you bring to it that makes it vibrant and alive or otherwise, dull and dead."

"Yeah, right! So here I am, all my old demons to keep me company," Kyle moaned.

"So, lay it on us, what's the connection?" Archie asked.

"Yeah, we're all ears," Blondie said.

"When I was a little boy, about four and a half, my mother had a serious nervous breakdown and had to be hospitalized. My dad was working full time as a herdsman for the state, so my older sister, brother, and I had to move to another town to live with my mother's family, two aunts and my grandparents. Another sister came later, when my mother finally came back and joined the extended family."

"So what, lots of kids go through stuff like that. What's the big deal; you're lucky they took you in. Besides, what's that got to do with anxiety?" Blondie asked.

"I don't know. All I can think of was the trauma of losing my Mom. Hell, right off, the day we moved, on the ride I got car sick two or three times and my uncle had to stop the car so I could get out to vomit!" Kyle replied.

"Nothing unusual about that," Archie said. Lots of people have motion sickness."

"Well, it's just now thinking back. I remember one of my aunts, when I did things she didn't like, she'd say, "you better behave if you ever want your mother to come home.""

At that, Archie's look softened and he shook his head.

"As though it was my fault that mom went away in the first place," Kyle continued. "Sometimes I cried, wondering what would become of me, but I didn't let anyone see me or know how I felt."

"What have letters got to do with all that? So, yeah, you probably were preoccupied, and consequently, you just didn't pay attention when you should have been learning English basics and how to spell. Then having never learned them, you were bound to feel diminished whenever confronted with writing and spelling. I guess it follows that you've got personal adjustment problems, but really, please don't lay them on us or the Land of Letters," Blondie said.

"I never said it was your fault. I was just trying to explain where I'm coming from. You know, childhood anxiety, like the letters just demonstrated," Kyle replied.

"Yeah, yeah, talk about self-centered and self-conscious, you take the cake," Blondie said.

"Definitely from the ME generation," Archie added.

"And sure fits the bill for an I. Maybe you'll even be desensitized and become less intimidated by letters and words, while you're here," Blondie said.

At that moment, M, with an Apostrophe, came up to Kyle and his two companions. Turning to Blondie while holding on to the Apostrophe, M said, "Can we borrow him," pointing to Kyle.

"Yeah, sure," Blondie replied.

"Wait just minute! What's going on?" Kyle asked.

"How about helping start a phrase," M asked.

"I wouldn't know where to begin," Kyle replied.

"Oh come-on. It'll be fun," M said, rather insistently.

Both A's urged Kyle, "Lighten up; go for it."

"Oh, alright!" Kyle exclaimed.

M, who looked so manly with his close, cut beard, brown eyes and deep voice, took Kyle by the left hand and they walked a short distance to an area in an adjacent field that looked to Kyle like a large piece of lined paper. PUZZLE, in his multi-colored garments, was fussing at some other letters, but he looked up as M, Apostrophe and Kyle arrived.

"You know the drill," PUZZLE said to M.

M then jumped onto a line pulling Kyle right along. At the very beginning of the line he let go and said to Kyle, "Don't move," as he slung Apostrophe over Kyle's left shoulder and stood next to him. Other letters followed in line, right to left.

On the left side of M, Kyle saw a strange transparent object. "Who's that?" he whispered to M.

"Just Space," M replied.

As Kyle looked down the line where he stood he realized he was leading the arrangement, I'M MY OWN MAN.

"What's this all about?" Kyle asked.***

"It's *Rejoinder*, one of PUZZLE's new creations," M replied.

Kyle looked away from M and was confronted with another line forming right in front of them, WHO IS SELF POSSESSED, he read.

"I get the sense this place is trying to tell me something." Kyle's tone was whiney.

"Get over yourself," M said. "Though we do espouse the saying, *if the shoe fits...*"

"This place has an answer for everything," Kyle rolled his eyes.

"You know, I've always heard, "You get out of things what you bring to them. Might be you should try being a little more positive. Who knows maybe you'll eventually become self-possessed," M replied.

"Oh, yeah, in my dreams," Kyle laughingly replied.

"You're a great one for irony, but don't laugh, stranger things have happened," M replied.

"Sure, with everything based on what PUZZLE does, incredulous, I'd say," Kyle replied.

"Isn't life a puzzle?" M asked.

"So I have a little doubt and a touch of ambivalence. I think that's okay. That's not to say it isn't disturbing," Kyle replied.

"All-in-all, though, I'd say you did pretty well for your first word game," M said.

Suddenly distracted, Kyle felt his limbs getting restless and different voices were broadcasting overhead.

"Dr. Angle, line three, Dr. Angle, line three," echoed in Kyle's ears like a cheap recording or a bad connection.

"Evette, see who that is will you," a voice said.

"It's the charge-nurse from station one, visitors for Kyle Wilson," another voice replied.

"God, that's me. Maybe they can get me," Kyle thought. "Can anyone hear me?" he tried to yell, but nothing was coming out!

"Now's as good a time as ever. Tell Bernese to bring them in," Dr. Angle said.

COMA

The phone was ringing just as Betsy Fleming called to her sister, Irene, "What lousy weather. Can you get that?"

"It's Molly Wilson, for you. She says it's an emergency," Irene called back.

"Hello, Molly. What's wrong?"

"It's Kyle, Betsy. There's been a terrible accident and he's in the Methuen hospital," her voice shaking.

"Oh, God! How bad is it? Will he be okay?" Betsy, a tall, lovely looking brunette, with a slender figure, cried.

Molly's voice was shaking, "It's not good. He's in a coma. That's all they would tell me. I'm going over there right away and I thought you'd want to come. I sure could use the moral support."

"Absolutely," Betsy didn't hesitate.

"I'll be there in ten minutes," Molly, replied.

On their way Betsy said, "God, I hope he's okay. He's a great guy. At least the roads seem okay now. Irene said they were terrible earlier this morning." Realizing what she'd just said, she added, "Oh God, he must have gone off the road or something, oh, how terrible!" she said, tearing up. "I don't know what I'll do, if anything bad happens."

"Don't go there. We don't know anything yet, so let's keep the faith. But, yeah, he really is a great guy," Molly replied.

"It's funny, when we met, I thought he was handsome - he is, too, but I didn't think he had much personality. Was I surprised on our first date! He just said funny, cute little things, jokes, you know, that told me he was engaged. As I've gotten to know him I realize how tuned in he is. He knows all my little foibles and he's a great kidder, sometimes a bit much, but I love him," Betsy said.

Molly and Betsy drove directly to the hospital. Taking the lead, Kyles' sister, Molly, hurriedly went to the admissions desk. "We're here to see my brother, Kyle Wilson."

"He's been moved to the ICU," the admissions clerk replied. "That's on the second floor, turn right when you get off the elevator."

On their way, confronting a floor sign, 'CAUTION WET FLOOR,' and smelling disinfectant, "I hate hospitals," Molly said, "They all smell and look the same."

At the ICU, nurses' station, they asked if they could see Kyle.

"He's in a coma and heavily sedated right now," the charge-nurse replied. "Let me check."

A nurse came out of a room down the hall and the ICU, charge-nurse called, "Bernese, these women are here to see Mr. Wilson."

Bernese introduced herself and said, "The doctor's in with him right now. He's been out since he arrived. It's a pretty serious head injury and the doctor has ordered a sedative, but I can take you there and you can see him and also meet Dr. Angle."

"Oh God," Betsy gasped, grasping Molly's arm as they entered the room.

Although Kyle's head was bandaged at the hairline, he still looked handsome, only he was twitching.

Kyle felt Dr. Angle holding his wrist and as the doctor checked his watch, he could hear, "His pulse is good," and then, "Hi, I'm Dr. Angle."

Before any introductions, Betsy blurted out. "Is he going to be okay, doctor?"

Kyle tried crying out, "Betsy I'm here, I'm here," but again, nothing came out.

"Truthfully, we never really know with these head-injury cases. It's helpful that he was transported right away and we started him on propranolol right off to help manage swelling in his brain, a common occurrence in these cases. We hope he'll come around, but it may be days or even weeks sometimes. We're monitoring him very carefully and I'm optimistic."

"Oh yeah, doc, that's just great news," Kyle thought in disgust, then thought, "God I'm trapped. Where the hell do I go from here?"

The doctor, turning to Bernese, said, "His pressure is a little high. Up the dosage to 2 mg propranolol when you hang the next drip and make sure to put it in the chart for the evening shift."

Leading Molly and Betsy out to the lounge area, Dr. Angle said, "I've already ordered a consult with Dr. Norris, the resident psychiatrist, and I think it would be a good idea for you both to meet him. His office is back down on the first floor. Please try not to worry. We'll notify you if there are any changes in his condition."

As Dr. Angle and Kyle's visitors walked away, Kyle felt himself drifting back to the Land of Letters…

Betsy grasped Molly's hand as they headed back to the first floor. "What do you think? It looks pretty serious, doesn't it," Betsy asked.

Molly, obviously shaken herself, tried consoling her, "He's so stubborn and tough in that quiet way of his, that nothing will keep him down."

"God, I hope his mind and memory are right if he does come around," Betsy said, continuing, "He's the last person that could live in a wheelchair having to relearn the three R's again. At this last remark, she started tearfully laughing, adding, he hated grammar school, you know, and said it was one of his big bugaboos, that he never learned spelling or proper grammar.

"So he's opened a big chink in that armor of his. He must really care about you. He doesn't share that with everyone," Molly replied.

After knocking, they heard, "Come in, come in." They walked in as Dr. Bradley Norris, a tall, thin, handsome man, with graying hair, horn-rimed-glasses and a mustache stood up from his desk and walked around to meet them. "Mrs. Wilson and Ms. Fleming, I'm pleased to meet you both and I'm glad you came down. Please have a seat. Bernese called and said you were on your way."

"So you've seen Kyle."

"Yes," they both nodded.

"Please don't be alarmed because he's unconscious. We sedate coma patients, sometimes quite heavily. It can be a big help in their recovery," Dr. Norris said.

"What happened to him? Do you have any idea of when he might wake up, doctor?" Molly asked.

Betsy, listening intently, was also taking the room in, looking at all the Doctor's diplomas, but mostly at an abstract painting of a head, with butterflies coming out of it, that unnerved her.

"Traumatic brain injury. This happens quite frequently in auto accidents. I don't want to alarm you, but it can be quite serious. You can be sure he'll get the very best care here," the doctor said.

"God, doctor, he's had enough problems early in his life and it seemed like he was finally getting his life together, with this wonderful woman at his side, gesturing to Betsy. His life is finally looking up, but now this," Molly said.

"What kind of problems?" Dr. Norris asked.

"Well, it's really not my place, but I guess given the current circumstances," Molly went on, "he got heavily into alcohol when he was a teenager. For a while we wondered if he'd ever grow up and get his act together."

"So he finally came around, did he?" the doctor asked.

"After years of therapy," Molly replied. "Of course, he still has issues, but Betsy is really making a man out of him."

Betsy spoke up, "What's it like, doctor? I mean what happens to patients like this? I hope he's not partially awake or something like you read about where people can't move a muscle but their minds are still churning. I worry he'd be so terrified, he's such a control freak, you know, when anything different happens and he has no control."

"It's different for everyone and it depends where, specifically, the brain is injured. In Kyle's case, I'm afraid his injury was largely sustained in the frontal lobes, where higher cognitive functions take place. This just means he may experience some impairment when he wakes," Dr. Norris said.

"It sounds terrible. Will he ever be himself again?" Betsy asked.

"This can often be helped with different therapies, including psychotherapy. Sometimes we've had patients who make personal psychological improvements while in coma and where actual dream work takes place. Patients can actually process issues dealing with their inner conflicts, something that

Kyle has at least partially come to grips with already, in his own earlier therapy. Fact is though, we just don't know. The unconscious is a mysterious place where events often appear, like dreams themselves, to defy logic."

"I'm so afraid he'll never wake up or that he won't know me when he wakes up," Betsy said, tears running down her cheeks.

"In most cases, patients do recover and are fully functional, and it's our job to help make sure that happens," Dr. Norris said. "Of course, your support will be critical too."

"Please try to keep a positive attitude. Dr. Angle and I will be carefully monitoring him and we'll certainly call if there are any developments."

Molly and Betsy thanked Dr. Norris and then left, holding on to each other, walking arm in arm.

IN A WORD, INSANITY

Meanwhile in the Land of Letters, "Yeah not bad at all for your first game," M repeated.

Kyle felt intimidated playing standard word games like Scrabble, because he was always unsure of his spelling, even though he had a strange way with words that he didn't quite understand. He did know that he had an unusual way of seeing puns in almost everything that people said.

"How about something more challenging?" M asked.

"I think I'll pass, I'm not very good at these things," Kyle said.

Blondie and Archie chuckled, along with a group of others standing nearby, saying, "You're not exactly a quick study, are you? But we realize you've had your difficulties with spelling! Anyway, why don't you give it a shot. What have you got to lose—maybe just a little false pride and that's a good thing, isn't it?"

"I don't think it's very nice to put people down. I'm not the greatest speller. So, what! You don't have to rub it in." But, feeling strangely cornered, Kyle said, "What's this new game?"

"PUZZLE has just set up a crossword in the field where you just played REJOINDER," Blondie said. "It's really the passage or bridge to the Land of Words. Actually, you're advancing quite well and we think it's time for you to matriculate and become a word."

"I thought I'd already crossed that bridge," Kyle said.

"Well, just not literally. Once you matriculate you're treated like a word and you won't be seeing the friends you've made here in the same light again!" Blondie said.

As Kyle looked out on a white field, he could see this arrangement of crisscrossing lines, inside a large square with numbers on two sides, with some blocked out squares and the other clear squares, big enough for letters to stand in.

"What are you waiting for? Jump in," Blondie said.

As Kyle looked at the Crossword, he could see all the clues on billboards nearby. At the same time, he could see other letters jockeying for position and apparently entering in groups.

Kyle turned to the Blondie saying, "I'm confused, I don't see any clues where an I like me can actually fit in."

"Look nobody said this was easy. It's a crossword and you'll have to find a clue where you fit in. Figure it out or you'll be stuck here!" Blondie said.

Kyle was reminded of when he was a little boy and his family's discussion about his risk for repeating the first grade, as he now urgently started poring over the clues. "Jesus Christ," Kyle muttered under his breath, as he finally noticed a clue that he thought might fill the bill (5 Across: God's announcement to Moses at the Burning Bush, in *Exodus*).

"I've got it! Nine letters," Kyle said out loud to himself. Then it dawned on him that he had to find the other letters to fill out the phrase.

"No wonder there's so much jockeying for position," he thought, as he started looking around for the other letters he had to corral. So, he rounded up two A's, two M's, one W, one H, and one O, but he also needed another I. This posed its own challenge when he asked an I nearby if he would join in his procession.

"What do you think I am?" the other I asked. I'm careful who I associate with! And besides, what's in it for me?"

Kyle felt flummoxed, but said, "We need you and it'll give you a chance to get across and join the others." Then half chuckling, "Could be you're doing God's work!"

"Oh, yeah, God's work, that's good! That's a pretty flimsy rationale, if I've ever heard one, but I'm sick of it here and I'm ready to move on. So, let's do it," the I said.

With that, Kyle's group of letters marched up to one of the Marshals, who looked them over very carefully and then asked, "What's your position?"

"5 Across," Kyle said.

"Okay, line up and proceed to your positions," the Marshal said.

With that the letters moved into their positions in the following order: I|AM|WHO|I|AM. The irony of this phrase was not lost on Kyle, who thought, "My God, where does it end, at every turn my integrity is either being questioned or challenged! First I'm confronted with childhood anxiety, then self-possessed and now, whatever. Everything in this place is a riddle!"

The Marshal checked them over very carefully, saying, "Okay," and then walked away, but Kyle could see the Marshal was checking the arrangement of letters following the 'W', at 8 Down in his group. There was a bit of a kerfuffle as a group of three letters were sent back to regroup, and then other letters filed into those positions. All of this seemed so tedious to him, and his mind drifted back to when he was a young boy in second grade and how bored he would get, just staring out the window, daydreaming and totally tuning out to the letters and words Ms. Noble, the teacher, was writing on the blackboard.

Kyle's focus was brought back to the crossword as it became completed and everyone was allowed to finish crossing. But Kyle could also see there were more Marshals checking them over as they were crossing. As he approached the officers, he could feel himself cringe with the thought of being apprehended. "Here we go again," he thought.

One of the officers said to him, "And your mode of travel, first—person singular?"

Before Kyle could speak, one of the other officers interjected, "Of course, can't you tell by his deportment?"

The first retorted, "Oh, I know. But one can't be too careful with all the different types, you know."

Once across the bridge, Kyle turned around and was amazed to see strange objects streaming across behind him. He could not recognize a single letter. Dumbfounded at such a change of appearances, he could only guess that it was due to the rapid pace of letters running to and fro.

"Come on, hurry up."

Kyle turned around to see himself confronted by this thing that had a perfectly round yellow body, wearing a waistcoat and cravat, resembling an emoji, but with arms and legs, a thick crop of red hair on top, big brown eyes, and a mouth that seemed to stretch across his upper body and that was set in what appeared to be a big wry smile. It was talking to him and looking right at him. "Will you please get going," it said exasperatedly. "We'll be late."

"Late for what?" Kyle asked.

"The Tournament of Words, naturally," it answered.

Since Kyle did not know what else to do, he walked off with his newfound acquaintance. "What are you?" Kyle asked.

"I'm a word," he answered.

"A word! Why if anything you look like an emoji to me," Kyle said.

"Don't let your tongue run away with your brains; *I am the word* WORD[1]. I embody all words, even myself. Sometimes this can be quite difficult, especially in a case such as yours. Why, if I wasn't careful, I wouldn't know who I was. An emoji of all things, after all these eons and you come along and size me up as just another pretty face! You've got some nerve!" He went on, as he ran his hand through his wavy red hair, "What's your shtick anyway and what brings you here?"

"I'm a librarian and I just came over from the Land of Letters, matriculated here as part of an unknown journey, and I'm confused already. Hell, things were finally going pretty good for me, then all of a sudden I find myself over there and now here in this strange place!"

Seeming to ignore Kyle, WORD just looked Kyle up and down. "You're lucky," he finally said, "you get to sit at the head table. Of course, we'll all be looking at you, but you won't mind. We usually don't see you anyway."

Kyle thought, "What's so unusual about that? That's the way it's always been. No one every pays me any mind." From his earliest years, he was shy, feeling he was different, and he believed nobody really thought much of him! But at these new comments Kyle looked down at himself. For an instant Kyle thought he was WORD, because it was WORD he was seeing. But as Kyle shifted his position, WORD slipped from view. I must be some sort of mirror, Kyle thought, bending his head over further. As he did this, some words at the top of the mirror came into view, but he was having difficulty reading them— they were backwards. Bewildered, he turned to WORD, asking

---

[1]   To help eliminate confusion character's names that are those of objects or abstract ideas will be capitalized.

what they said. WORD curtly replied, "Can't you read? It says Vanity Mirror."

Kyle thought back when he was seven or eight – the time he had tried repairing an electrical extension cord, but had taped the bare wires incorrectly, causing it to blow a fuse. Of course, the lights and refrigerator had gone off, and even though the family didn't scold him and had even tried to console him, none of that could offset their laughing at him. He had felt terrible and had gone off by himself and cried, his self-confidence crushed! Again, in this current moment, he felt the same way, totally unsure of himself. But now as an adult he asserted himself, saying, "What the hell is going on? I don't even know where I am, much less what I'm supposed to do."

"Just because I embody all words doesn't mean I'm all things to everyone. Mind you, I do my best to be evenhanded, but you really have to paddle your own canoe over here," WORD said.

"That's not very friendly. Don't you make allowances for novices?" Kyle said.

"Up to a point, but look at it from my point. I represent words like IRASCIBLE, INSCRUTABLE, NIHILISTIC, BOMBASTIC, CHAUVINISTIC, SILLY, FOOLISH, STUPID... the list goes on. I do have a family life, you know, and I'm quite sociable, rubbing elbows whenever I can. But if it makes you feel any better I've had my own identity issues over the years. I remember way back when I was first uttered, and then in my naiveté being shocked to find myself in letterform on stone tablets and later moving to vellum, then on to paper, and God knows what or where else – oh yeah and now an emoji, instinctively straightening his waistcoat and cravat! Additionally, I'm now shepherding you around. I don't mean to put you off, we really do welcome you, and believe it or not, you'll catch on," WORD said.

"Thank you, that helps," Kyle said. "A family, really? You mean there's a Mrs. WORD? So, who's the lucky lady?"

"I don't usually tell others because ETYMOLOGY, well, she's quite private when it comes to her personal life and prefers to use her maiden, surname. Gosh, it seems like only yesterday but we tied the knot way back when. I was just coming into my own. Now look at all the words that have followed and she can tell you all about anyone of them, where they hail from and what they're about."

"Wow, all this time I thought English words were gender neutral. What about all the other words? How do they get on?" Kyle asked.

WORD, acting fussed at the question and while adjusting his cravat, said, "Look at your own English-speaking world; do you know who's doing what with whom? Seems like anything goes, gender be damned. It's no different here, the apple doesn't fall very far from the tree, unlike our Latin language cousins, who seem at least to present an attempt at gender identity. So yeah, there are some unlikely matchups here, but they remain pretty much under wraps, or as you would say, in the closet. Privacy is something that we respect here, in the Land of Words."

"Okay, we're almost there. Make sure you sing out who you are when it's your turn."

"What now," Kyle moaned.

WORD was nonchalant. "Oh, it's nothing really. It's roll call, that's all. VOCABULARY wants to check his flock, a 'must' before every Tournament. I just dote on roll-call. It's one of the few times that I get embodied. This one should be especially good. I understand there will be quite a turnout. VOCABULARY told me he's expecting 10,000 or more!"

WORD nudged Kyle. "Get ready," he said.
VOCABULARY pointed to HYSTERIA, who looked something like a vanity mirror, but with frosted glass.

HYSTERIA sang out, "Hysteria!"

VOCABULARY pointed to Kyle and Kyle said, "I."

It was to be a little while before WORD got to say his piece. Kyle just looked around. In all the clatter of chairs moving around and the din of voices across the auditorium, he was surprised at the different appearances. VOCABULARY looked like a book, but with arms and legs and wavy blond hair, and with a picture of WORD on his covers. Wearing granny glasses, he looked very officious while running around, checking on this, that, and the other.

Kyle tried several times to glean some information from HYSTERIA, who was on his left, but he guessed by HYSTERIA's very nature it was difficult for him to say anything without getting upset. While he was taking it all in, his mind drifted back to earlier times and his shrink. He remembered the early sessions when he was hospitalized after trying to commit suicide. He had felt so lost, without purpose and out of place in the world. He remembered asking the shrink what the course of treatment would be and when would he ever start feeling better about himself. The shrink had said he would likely notice some changes in six months, but that in the world of psychoanalysis change is measured in years. Now, in this strange world, he felt that same strange sense of isolation and being out of place that he'd thought was behind him. Were all these letters and words the manifestation of his verbal insecurities from his childhood? And how was he to deal with all this now—a captive in a virtual world?

As Kyle had this turn inward, he looked to his right, to another word, I-BEAM, who looked something like a proper I should look. Sensing Kyles' mood, he asked, "Hey, Buddy, how's it going? You look like you could use a friend. Is everything okay?"

"God, this place is so different and I feel so out of place. What's going on? Do you know?"

All this while I-BEAM had been preening himself right in front of Kyle, but Kyle guessed that this was his new station in life, being an 'I' and all and he tried to appear oblivious to I-BEAM'S vanity.

I-BEAM told Kyle not to fuss, that after roll call, they would be free to roam around, find their seats and get settled.

"That's easy for you to say," Kyle said, still confused, in a quandary and seeing nothing festive about his current situation.

"Take it easy, man. It's only words getting up to their usual activities. You know, palaver is the name of the game here. Don't be afraid, just speak up when you've got something to say and you'll fit right in. You know, 'fake it 'till you make it'," I-BEAM said.

"Thanks, that makes me feel better," Kyle said, glancing around. He did know where to sit, but this was overshadowed by the most unusual atmosphere. Some things were what they seemed to be. Other things seemed to be things they were not. And some things Kyle thought should be present didn't appear to be there at all.

Kyle turned to WORD with an air of bewilderment.

WORD nodded. "Yes, everything is here; it's part of what makes up IMAGINATION."

"But, I haven't seen that either," Kyle interjected, "and what's more, I thought this was the Land of Words."

WORD looked at Kyle with a rather puzzled expression and said, "Use your own imagination, will you! Can you think of a better place for the Land of Words?"

"Well, no, I guess not. But it isn't just that; it's everything. Just VOCABULARY'S appearance alone, sends my head spinning," Kyle bemoaned.

"That's not unusual in the Land of Words," WORD replied and, with that, he pointed to a large mirror that encompassed a very small mirror. The small mirror looked just like Kyle. "That's PERSON," WORD said.

Kyle was dumbfounded and asked WORD what was going on.

WORD replied, "When he looks at you he embodies you and when you look at him you embody him."

At that, Kyle looked down at himself. There was PERSON with Kyle, appearing as a vanity mirror, on the front of him, looking down at himself embodying PERSON.

With a knot welling up in his gut, Kyle turned to WORD and in barely audible tones said, "Jesus this is one mixed up place!"

"Oh, you'll get used to that here. It's a perfectly natural state," WORD replied.

Just then Kyle noticed a thing that resembled a nose, with black hair on the top and a mustache underneath coming towards them. Now, who's this?" he asked.

WORD casually replied, "Oh, that's OBSCURE."

"I would think he should be OBVIOUS," Kyle said.

"Exactly," replied WORD. "That's what makes him OBSCURE."

"Goddamn!" Kyle exclaimed.

Through all the noise of words talking, finding seats and taking their chairs, a faintly heard pounding of a gavel echoed across the auditorium, and the area became very still. CONCENTRATION, a bright light bulb, was calling the Tournament to order.

Kyle took his place at the head table, between CONCENTRATION and THOUGHT, a warm glowing light bulb. CONCENTRATION stood up and addressed the group. "For those of you who don't know the rules, there will be 26 delegates, one elected from each group. The one of those who tells the best story, chosen by a voice vote, shall be deemed the winner. We'll start with the A's." Continuing, he asked, "Have the A's chosen a delegate?"

"Yes," they chorused.

ALONE stepped forward. His deportment was that of a number 1. Addressing the group, he began, "CONCENTRA-TION, I, THOUGHT, and other words, I have been penned many times, and a hundred as many have I sat on the tip of some tongue waiting to be finally uttered. I usually depict a rather common human situation. But please let me elaborate; as we all know words are such fickle things. And, of course, I must distinguish myself from my close relative, LONELY, who usually depicts the state of being dejected by the awareness of being alone. However, being alone is often a welcome situation where one has time to collect one's thoughts in the absence of interruptions. On the other hand, I do acknowledge to being lonely at times, and I have to say I can't ever remember being more 'lonely' than the time I was beside myself with WORRY; that is if you can picture a number 11 standing by a crumpled ball of paper, that never looked the same twice-Oh that WORRY, always sporting a new wrinkle! But second only to this is a story of my presence that lends itself to a different side of verbiage."

Leaning backwards, as on one heel, and extending his arms, ALONE ebulliently exclaimed, "We've all heard of the hostess with the mostest, but being ever the contrarian, I call my story:

HOST WITH THE LEAST

I had been sort of a sidekick with this host that was a rather reclusive person. But you know how things are with words – always wanting to move on. Anyway, this host really had an imagination and a vocabulary to fill it. Well, I didn't know what was good for me. One morning, my host was talking with this other person, who really looked like he would be intriguing to visit. I couldn't believe it, but, just as I was looking the prospective host over, I was called to duty. It felt good to be rolling off the tip of a tongue again. That's when I should have guessed it – the person my host had been talking to wasn't listening. It took every bit of strength I had to get across to him, a foolish move on my part to be sure. Why, there wasn't enough room in that host's imagination to bring a period along. I was caught by my own devices on a desert of superficiality. Oh, there were other words there, all right, but not the kind I usually associate with. VANITY, GREED and HATE prevailed. I was left to a life of solitude, poetic justice for a word such as myself. This Host and I traveled the cabarets, the streets of evil, and chased the favors of the loosest women.

Caught in the web of this host's childish personality, I was sure I would never be mentioned, nor likely penned – he barely wrote. And as surely as alone as I was, so also was he unaware of my presence. His shallowness seemed so excessive as to render him completely spontaneous and incapable of feeling the slightest twinge of the more elevating human passions. Alone and bearing my cross in despair, committed to martyrdom by stupidity, I stood awaiting the fate of eternity's timeless fancy. But, fate was to smile on me once again. This *host with the least* was talking with someone. The other person was having a difficult time of it, surely through no fault of his own. My host's incredible reply to a question was, 'What, me? I'm never alone.' Thus, as I had been snared so likewise was I spared!"

There was a very mild applause as ALONE concluded and took his seat.

"Jesus, what's the big deal," Kyle said. "Hell, when I was a kid I was left to myself for hours at a time." Kyle could hear his grandfather now, especially on Saturdays and in the Summer. "Inside the house, that's no place for a boy, get your arse outside, you little whelp!"

So, in his early childhood years Kyle would go out to play by himself and if you had looked for him you would have found him with his imaginary friends and maybe with his little model gas-station, happily lost in his world of play. He felt okay around the adults and siblings in his extended family, but he was basically very shy and only had a few neighborhood friends that he kept at a safe distance.

Turning to THOUGHT Kyle said, "I guess I'm missing something. Who isn't alone a good share of the time? It's only when you get that terribly despondent feeling that you can't cope with something that it falls squarely on you. Then the sense of being alone turns into loneliness, feelings of panic, and how you are going to deal with whatever it is that's coming down on you."

At the mention of all this, Kyle started feeling lonely, much like when he was a little five-year-old! His mother having been taken to a state hospital because of her nervous breakdown and his father staying behind for his work, he often felt lonely living with his mother's family and grandparents. In this confused period, he had missed his mother terribly. He hadn't connected the dots then, and wondered if he had been at least partly responsible for his mother's leaving. Again, he thought of his aunt, who said he had to be good if he wanted his mother to ever come home, sometimes even crying and wondering what was going to become of him. Eventually his mother did come home, but all this turmoil left him unsure of his place at home and he became quite self-conscious and very fearful of rejection by others.

In the Land of Letters, now the Land of Words, it seemed so strange to experience those old feelings.

"Childhood anxiety—yeah that's very real," he thought; because he now felt like he had in those bygone years, he wasn't at all sure of what or who he really was or how he was supposed to act. Somehow, he also knew, spelling and grammar were a part of these insecurities.

THOUGHT interrupted his reverie, saying, "Oh, so, now you're an authority on what it means to be alone. Maybe you'd like to step up and tell us all the particulars."

"No, of course not! Isn't anyone allowed to comment without being called out?" Kyle felt fully in his right to protest.

These asides by Kyle and THOUGHT were interrupted by CONCENTRATION, who banged his gavel, and looking in the direction of the B's said, "And, for the B's who will it be?"

A large round piece of glass rolled toward the podium. Its transparency was of such clarity as to immediately draw one's attention to it.

"Who's that?" Kyle asked.

"Oh, that's BEAUTY," THOUGHT replied.

"BEAUTY?" Kyle queried. "Why, if it were any less clear, I wouldn't know it was even there. And what's more, when I look at it, I don't see anything that wasn't really there before."

"Maybe that's the idea," conjectured THOUGHT.

Kyle, still feeling confused, alone and very much an outsider, lapsed into a reverie, how beautiful Betsy had looked on the first day that he met her. She was there at the church he had started going to after he stopped drinking. It was social hour after service. She was setting up the refreshments. She had come up to him, sensing he was new, and had offered him a coffee. It made him smirk to think about how disarming she was trying to be, in her Sunday attire.

"Yes, thank you," he had said. She certainly was beautiful with beautiful black tresses, but underneath her fresh and lively appearance he could also see she was shy. The way she demurred at his offer, for her to join him for coffee, pleased him. He preferred people who weren't too forward. But then a crushing sense of alienation came over him that brought him back to his current situation. "Why am I here," he thought. "It isn't as if I haven't gone over all this stuff in therapy. And now beauty; haven't I resolved anything?" he asked himself. "Forget about Betsy! It's all this other crap and what the hell can I do about it? How will I ever put this stuff behind me, not to mention, these letters and words?"

BEAUTY was at the podium addressing the group, "Friends, it gives me great pleasure to be here, perhaps because I see so much of myself in each of you. But to get on with my real purpose, I am about to tell you a tale of unique nature, and also one of the commonplace. I call it:

I WAS WHERE I WASN'T

Many centuries ago, I was residing in this thorny plant near the doorway of a peasant's cottage. One sunny day, when the peasant's mind wasn't troubled with the necessities of life, he spied the growth where I resided.

"Lucrecia," he called. His wife came running.

"What is it, Papa?" she asked.

"Look, Lucy, have you ever seen such ugliness?"

"No, it looks evil," she replied.

Giuseppe grabbed at it, intent on destroying it. "Ah-h!" he blurted out in pain. "It has teeth that carry the devil's own spirit with them."

Lucy cried, "Oh, Papa, let it be! Surely, you will bring evil spirits upon us."

Thus they retired into the cottage, with Giuseppe licking his wounds.

I don't know if it was that or what it could have been. But as the days with warmth of sunlight filled my life, I began to feel strange, as though I was striving for some ultimate identity. Of course, as you all know I could never see myself anyway, except as I am manifested in others and other things.

One day as Giuseppe was passing by, he called, "Lucy, quick come see."

Lucy, looking at me, gasped – hand on mouth, "Papa, surely not from the devil's own handiwork has such beauty come."

"Oh my Lucy," Giuseppe murmured. "Is it not the strangest red that you have ever seen?"

"Ah, Papa, it is red – not quite – but yes, it is, I think, a rose."

A moment of silence, interspersed with ooh's and ah's, was followed by a standing ovation.

"So we end up with a rose, the archetypical symbol of beauty and love," Kyle pointed out. "Everyone knows beauty is in the eye of the beholder. What's the point?"

THOUGHT spoke up, "I think he's trying to say beauty is everywhere; you just have to look for it."

"Oh, I get it. There's a Pollyanna under every rock."

"For Christ's sake, lighten up, will you," THOUGHT retorted. You know WORD and I would never have become friends if we were as rigid as you make life out to be. Talk about bringing your baggage with you. You'd do well to try and be a little more spontaneous. Life's a lot more fun that way. Back in the beginning, when we became friends, and we didn't know everyone, we would play games, trying to identify new friends. Other times we would just hang out with others of our kind. You know, a little palaver goes a long way in calming the savaged soul." He pushed his sparse, blond hair over his receding forehead as he wrapped up his argument.

Starting to reply, Kyle was interrupted by CONCENTRATION banging his gavel. He called to the C's. "Let us see what the C's can do."

A large shiny object waddled forward. Upon the most casual observation, one could easily see it was a gem of the finest quality. As he stepped into the lights, standing at the podium, you could barely see his arms and legs, not to mention his wavy, silver hair.

THOUGHT looked amazed when Kyle asked about the representative of the C's. "Funny thing about you I's. You're so terribly egotistical that you fail to recognize, through your own lack of it, the very thing you are now looking at. In fact, I have often wondered why they call it COMMON-SENSE when something as priceless and with as many facets is surely very rare."

COMMON-SENSE began addressing the crowd, "Friends, I thought CONCENTRATION and other words have, at times in the past, demonstrated a keen awareness of my being. It is, however, today that I have chosen a different narrative to demonstrate my existence. I call it, not so incidentally:

NONSENSE

Once upon a time, there was this beautiful land – a haven of supposed liberty. But this land also believed that some of the other places in the world should have some of the pleasures it was enjoying.

When these other countries resisted the prospects of the supposed liberty, this great land sent forth its armies to purge the infidels of their stubbornness and stupidity.

At first, the people of this great land (as affluent a bunch as you have ever seen) seemed oblivious to the killing of the alien men, women, and children, and their own country's young men. But slowly, the citizens of this aggressor's country began to cry out that they were sick and tired of destroying their only real wealth and the wealth of the countries they were supposedly purging. Many demonstrations ensued, but alas the president and his closest advisors seemed oblivious to such human conscience. But, gradually I took the opportunity to slip into the president's palace. Well, when the president at last got a taste of common-sense, he decided he could stand an earful. He thereupon sent his best advisor, a supposedly highly educated man, in search of more of the same. A most fortunate decision, I can assure you. For had the president gone himself, he probably would have grabbed the first citizen he came across, turned him upside down and shaken him until his pockets were empty. That's common-sense to most politicians, but as most of you know, common-sense is not found in anyone's pockets, and it doesn't necessarily come with an education. In fact, common-sense is very much like our elusive friend, OBSCURE.

The advisor's education served him well, causing him to revisit his former beliefs, in hopes of gaining a new perspective. Somewhere in this search he met with quite a bit of success. He was a wiser man when he returned to his homeland. Common-sense was in such abundance that he managed to give the president an earful and, I guess, a few generals a bellyful. At any rate, they made peace and that's one thing that does make sense.

COMMON-SENSE was shining after resounding crescendos of applause, with shouts of encore.

"Yeah, that story makes sense, I guess, but what's the big deal," Kyle said.

"Oh sure, like so many others, you take COMMON-SENSE for granted, but I think you'll find it's so often the primary ingredient that's missing in many snafus, big and small," THOUGHT replied.

CONCENTRATION restored order, and he nodded to COMMON-SENSE, a gesture for him to encore.

COMMON-SENSE positioned himself in such a manner that his sheer radiance stilled the thunderous applause. "Fellow words, you do me a great honor. But it is I, above all, who must know when I have spoken enough. With this thought I leave you, respectfully, COMMON-SENSE."

THOUGHT was glowing a little brighter than usual.

"Are you all right?" Kyle asked.

"Oh, yes," he replied. "I was just thinking of those last words. It left me feeling that I, too, could have a little common-sense!"

"Shouldn't you be careful about having those kinds of thoughts? Don't you words ever worry about losing your sense of identity?"

THOUGHT laughed, as he joked, "Oh heavens no, but elevating all the same. Although I'm known to be bright, on occasion, I have also become irrational and stupid."

"Are you trying to confuse me?" Kyle asked.

"As I said a moment ago, lighten up. Fake it 'till you make it, and you'll catch on, eventually."

Kyle slipped back into his reverie. "God, what a place, I sure worry what I'm supposed to do or say all the time, especially in this place. I don't understand how, but maybe this place will somehow desensitize me, but it's not a whole lot of fun."

CONCENTRATION banged his gavel restoring order, also getting Kyle's attention.

A delegate had been chosen from the D's. From their ranks, a figure, resembling an index-finger, dexterously moved towards the speaker's station. As he moved he was swaying, as if in a gentle breeze, while at the same time murmuring a steady stream of yes's and no's.

When Kyle asked CONCENTRATION who this was and what it was doing, he got no reply, so he turned to THOUGHT, who conveyed to him that it was DISCRIMINATION and that CONCENTRATION was caught up in a sense of the word and that he was just discriminating, as we all do almost every waking moment of our lives.

DISCRIMINATION, at the podium, was addressing the audience, "My friends, I stand before you by choice alone. While I believe this story has individual merit, I'm not telling it solely for that purpose. I hope when you hear it you will discriminate to the fullest extent possible. I know this will be difficult for some of you. And perhaps there are those of you, such as BIASED and PREJUDICE, that shall choose not to listen at all. This choice I must leave to each of you, but whose end product shall be the result of discrimination. Hence my story:

LIKE IT OR NOT

The Bluegrass Country is especially beautiful in the summer months, a sad state of affairs for a man of Henry Benken's sensitivities. This man who had blossomed in that very countryside and had sated every appetite a man can from the bluegrasses' bounties. Oh, he had gone away awhile and studied law and easily entered the Phi Beta Kappa society of the eastern establishment, but his roots were deep in the southern lifestyle, and it was back to the ham and grits as soon as the law would allow for a junior attorney in those environs. A thriving law practice and finally a county judgeship brought him the esteem that goes only to judges and men of power. But, Henry was cut from a mold that did not let him succumb to flattery or drown himself in glory. He had turned countless pages, pursuing a wide range of interests, and he had waded through volumes that would turn a librarian to other pursuits.

Benken came to be known as the most discriminating man in the valley. People came from distant parts of the state to partake of the luxury of conversation with such a learned man.

But, alas, as time catches up with all of us, so also did it catch up with Henry Benken. As the pages of time slowly turned, the bluegrass and the valley that he loved slipped from his view. And yet he was still a wealthy man, for he had memories of thoughts, ideas, and sights that now could serve him well.

One county away from the judge's was the town of Cannonville, a poor man's town, for all of the bluegrass and the rich Kentucky countryside. It was a black man's town trying to shake off the tradition of white oppression. But, all of this hadn't stopped George Washington Smith from acquiring the finer things of life, the finer things to George, that is. He had hacked himself a sizeable piece of education out of that intellectually sterile community, the kind that comes with pain, sorrow and love. There wasn't a thought that had escaped his imagination. He became as ardent a conversationalist as any man in those parts. He was the consoling brother and intellectual confidant of his race.

However, as with the unfortunate judge, the ravages of time had stolen from George his eyesight.

It happened one day that the judge was traveling with his son to visit a relative in a part of the state that was to take him directly through Cannonville. The vehicle the judge was traveling in developed some sort of difficulty and it was decided a stop in Cannonville would be necessary.

Upon stopping, John Benken, the judge's son and driver, escorted his father to the only tavern in town in order that the judge might refresh himself on that hot summer day. John guided his father to a table inside and left in search of repairs.

"It must have been meant for men to imbibe in hot weather," thought George, as he was escorted to the stoop of the town's tavern. His escort left him there, knowing that George's previous excursions would lead him safely inside. As George stepped inside and took his favorite spot, the judge was startled to alertness as he felt the table jiggle to George's bumpy seating. "I'm Henry Benken," he said. "Excuse my staying seated, but I'm slightly indisposed at the moment."

"Quite all right, George Smith here, and glad to make your acquaintance, sir."

For a full two hours, these two men wrapped themselves in each other's thoughts. Delicate duels of conversation transpired.

The judge's son returned and helped him to the repaired and waiting vehicle. On the way, he whispered, "Father, that was a black man you were talking to."

"Come, son, don't you think I know that? At my old age, what's the difference, black or white? You know you can't tell a book by its cover."

"George," the innkeeper gasped, upon the judge's exit, "That was a white man you were talking to."

"Sam, you know better than to question my motives and actions. You see, it's the contents, not the vessel that makes cut flowers grow. At my old age, I'm lucky to only see through the mind's eye and this time I came up smelling roses."

DISCRIMINATION'S story brought only mild applause, and CONCENTRATION had order restored with little effort. Then, with no seeming surprise to anyone with the exception of Kyle, CONCENTRATION stood up and said, "I now declare the Tournament to be over. We all know the W's will pick the winner."

Kyle, turning to THOUGHT, protested: "This place is crazy. Everything is different from the way you would expect it to be."

THOUGHT casually replied. "That may be so in your case. But, if you ever tried expecting the unexpected, you would then be able to expect anything! Besides, why continue doing something when you're sick of it? CONCENTRATON is weary, I'm tired of thinking and don't you ever just get sick and tired of being you?"

"Stop," shouted Kyle. "I can't be anything different than I am. Just the way I think is part of me. How do you expect me to understand such contrary and insane thoughts?"

THOUGHT replied, "Thinking like that keeps you from growing and changing. Just by the nature of being an I, one might conclude your problem is identity. If you were really sure of what and who you are, you could relax and not worry about being anything else."

Again, Kyle felt very subdued, thinking, "I wonder if I'll ever put this doubt behind me and where is all this leading anyway?"

"Enough!" said THOUGHT, "Let's get going. You may stay the night at my place."

THOUGHT and Kyle strolled off together.

AT HOME WITH THOUGHT

Kyle was amazed at the surroundings of the areas he and THOUGHT were passing. Again, hauntingly familiar, "I'm in the college library. Most of the houses and buildings look like different books, and they're sitting on the strangest looking shelves and in the weirdest stacks I've ever seen," he thought.

"Well, here it is." THOUGHT stopped in front of a beautiful structure where the stack opened up, looking like a street, and Kyle could see the shelf was really a driveway.

"It certainly is beautiful."

"Yes," said THOUGHT, "I think it's the nicest place in the area, genuine leather bindings and a special silk interior."

"Wow. By the way, what's that on the roof?"

"Oh, yes, that never did stand out too well," THOUGHT replied. "It's the title to the estate—that is, *Spell Bound*."

"*Spell Bound,* what a strange title. God, this is unsettling. It reminds me of Ms. Noble, as well as Ms. Gilmore, my third-grade teacher?" Kyle thought.

With a bowing motion and a gesture of his right hand, THOUGHT directed Kyle up the path to his abode.

When Kyle stepped inside, everything immediately changed and he was shocked to see himself lying in a hospital bed, surrounded by white coats and he again heard, "Nonresponsive. TBI. Bernese, hang 1 mg IV propranolol, every six hours..."

One blink and the bewildered Kyle was back amongst the letters, and keenly aware that he had been there before. THOUGHT was nowhere to be found. The shadow of other letters appeared in the background. He approached, then blurted, "Have you seen anything that looks like a warm glowing light bulb?"

"Tut, tut. Have you forgotten your manners?"

"Suddenly I'm back in second grade," Kyle realized.

"Okay, okay, I get it," he said. "I'm an I, if you please, and I'm delighted to see you THOUGHT."

A moment of silence was followed by a deep sigh from Kyle, as he questioned, "How come I never see things until after they have happened?"

"Oh, that's just a carryover from your more human side. But you are improving," THOUGHT replied. "You have to remember that things very often look different upon a second look. Why sometimes I've looked at the same thing a thousand different ways, only to see a thousand different things. But, all this stuff is old hat, let's move on."

"Easy for you to say, but give me a break," Kyle said.

On this note, THOUGHT and Kyle took up their trek through the Land of Letters.

"God," Kyle thought, "I'm doing this all over again! It's an out-of-body experience, what the hell. Like it wasn't crazy enough the first time? Oh, hell, I'll just roll with it, I guess."

His sister, Betsy, and a figure in a white coat were at his side.

More propranolol.

Then it was back across the bridge to the Land of Words.

Kyle again lost track of his friend. But, he thought, "I won't be so easily fooled this time." Looking around, he noticed a light bulb not too far from him. He ran over to it, saying, "Figured you would fool me, didn't you THOUGHT?"

"Just who do you think you are, running around disturbing everyone?" the light bulb asked. "I'm CONCENTRATION; I suppose you think I'm THOUGHT because it's lighter out than usual. Is that supposed to make me any dimmer? I guess if you were in the dark you would probably mistake THOUGHT for me, just because he looked a little brighter. Don't you ever think before you speak?"

"What the hell?" Kyle shouted. "You guys make it really tough to get along here."

"Well, that's okay this time, but please pay attention. If you're looking for THOUGHT, he's over there." CONCENTRATION pointed to a very dim looking light bulb.

"This place is so strange. I think one thing, but it's usually just the opposite. Reminds me of times in the past when I made assumptions that were totally wrong too," Kyle thought.

The first day of boot camp. After being assembled into a squadron and listening to the first dos and don'ts of military life, the group was told to enter the barracks and pick a bunk. Everyone was told to first remove their shoes before entering.

Kyle, like his fellow recruits, dutifully removed his shoes, but unlike everyone else, he left his shoes on the stoop, immediately outside the doorway. He'd heard this is what people did in many other parts of the world. The sergeant, eagerly awaiting a scapegoat, called Kyle out, and deftly flung his shoes, under another billet, making Kyle crawl after them.

"Am I never to get past these kinds of situations? Where does it end?" Kyle thought, as he went over to his friend.

THOUGHT said nothing and the two of them continued on their way. They went by the Tournament in the Land of Words, on to Chapter IV, on into THOUGHT'S home, continuing to where they had gone through the Land of Letters, into the hospital, then the Land of Words and onto Chapter IV.

All of a sudden, Kyle started screaming and then yelling at WORD, "Why, we haven't gone very far at all! We're right where we are!" Tears were running down his face.

"That's about all any of us can say, but it's hardly worth crying about. For most of us, life is a reflexive process of looking backward and then moving forward, hopefully learning something about ourselves in the process," replied THOUGHT.

"You have no idea. I've poured my whole life out in a shrink's office. It wasn't easy, you know. Half the time I felt so dependent because I couldn't unravel the problems and mystery of my own life; the other half, it seemed our combined goal was for me to become more independent. Anyway, talk about setting me up for a schism; this place takes the cake for that. Hell, now I'm covering ground that seems to be almost intentionally familiar, and like I should know how to respond, but then I miss the boat, only to be caught up short again."

"Look, when you think you have to have the answer for everything, you're just setting yourself up to fail," THOUGHT said. "One can't know everything; everybody drops the ball sometimes. So don't beat yourself up; think of these things as experiences, you know, you are where you are in life, and stop the musterbation."

"What the hell are you talking about and how does sex come into this?" Kyle asked.

"Mus-ter-ba-tion! Not masturbation. It's commonly used to imply one is driven by inner impulses, like 'I must know this' or 'I must do that.' Otherwise one might think of this as, the dictates of the *Should*. I should be better than this or I should not mind that."

"In my mind, that's you – striving to be a super human – and that's a tough road to go down. Seems like you got a pretty good case of these mind games."

"Try a little self-acceptance; you'll find life's a lot easier to take. Also, as far as your journey today goes, I might point out that none of us is very far removed from the womb upon our death, but most of us are seldom fortunate enough to see what you have seen. We so often think that we have made great strides, when in all actuality each day is just a repeat of every other day. Because the days look different to us, we think they are different. Should we, but for a moment, lift the cloak that disguises the days we would find nothing but a continuum..."

"Look, a good night's rest and you'll feel a lot better about all this."

"Oh, God, that would be a welcomed relief," Kyle sighed.

"The guest room is just down the hallway to your right," THOUGHT said.

"So I get to retrace my journey here, in this screwball world, in your home, and the next move is the guest room and the future. First looking backward and now forward. What the hell, I guess I shouldn't be surprised."

Kyle wandered down the hall, walked into the room and climbed into bed, feeling subdued. He soon drifted off.

But there was no such thing as sleep. THOUGHT was saying, "WORD is coming by in a little bit and we'll have a few drinks. You know, just a little something to help us relax and shut out the cares of this world."

"I can't, I don't drink," Kyle blurted out.

Suddenly, like his reaction to *a few drinks* when he was taking Antabuse, he felt his skin crawling and bile rising from his gut as he heard,

"Calling Dr. Angle, ICU – Room 3. Calling Dr. Angle, ICU – Room 3..."

"Bernese, what happened?" Dr. Angle asked.

"Yeah, what the hell's happening now?" Kyle thought, as he heard the doctor, and not making any connection to his prior interaction with THOUGHT.

"The monitor went off when his heart rate and pressure spiked. He's very agitated and I think he might start to seize," Kyle heard Bernese say.

"You've checked his vitals?" Dr. Angle asked.

"Yes, Doctor."

"You've hung the increased drip?"

"Yes, Doctor."

"Could be a reaction to the propranolol. History of alcoholism, according to his chart. I'll check with Dr. Norris. But his vitals are in normal limits now, so, just keep monitoring and alert me to any changes," Dr. Angle said and then walked away.

HAIR OF THE DOG

"You don't drink? Come on, just a few. We'll let our hair down."

In walked WORD. "Hello, hello, he said, shaking hands with THOUGHT and Kyle.

"Will our neurotic I be joining us?"

"Who are you to call me neurotic?" Kyle angrily replied.

"Get over yourself, will you? In my mind, all I's are neurotic, by their very nature. They are self-centered and self-indulgent, not to mention deeply conflicted," WORD said.

"I won't say it doesn't apply, but couldn't you be a little more diplomatic?" Kyle said.

"Don't take him personally. WORD just calls 'em as he sees them," THOUGHT said.

Kyle's mind was going, "God, will I ever put this doubt behind me? Where is all this leading?"

"Enough!" said THOUGHT. "Let's get going."

The three companions left THOUGHT's home and walked outside around to a corner bar with an old, worn sign, **SLATTERY'S,** hanging out front. "Coincidence," Kyle first thought, but he was taken aback when inside he was confronted with the dingy tavern that he used to frequent.

"Calm down; It's just a few pops," THOUGHT said.

"Yeah, nothing to worry about, just 'a hair of the dog that bit you'!" WORD said, ordering two Rémy Martins.

"You guys have no idea! I can't! I haven't had a drink in almost 30 years!" Overcome by the musty aromas of spilled liquors, ales and beers, Kyle was whining.

"Oh come on, one drink won't hurt you. What the hell man, lighten up and enjoy life," THOUGHT said.

"Alright, alright, Allen's Ginger Brandy, on the rocks," Kyle said, wiping the sweat from his brow. "This place gives me the creeps. God, talk about a devil's bargain. I'd like to have a nickel for every one of these I've ever tossed back."

A warm glowing sensation came over Kyle, as the liquor reached his stomach. Suddenly, he was alive, in control and free of doubt.

"I'll have another, JIM, and a bottle of *Bud*," Kyle said absentmindedly, to the bartender, who looked like a barrel, and then, "Sorry, about the name. I wasn't thinking."

"That's it, how'd you guess?"

"My head was somewhere else and you just really reminded me of a bartender from years ago."

"Get a load of this guy," WORD said.

"In for a penny, in for a pound!" Kyle replied, sucking down his second shot and perusing the bottles on the shelves behind the bar.

"More like old habits die hard," THOUGHT added.

"Whatever, Kyle said, adding, "So is this a regular hangout for you guys?"

"Hangout, I don't know, but, yeah we come here frequently. The prices are good, nobody's on our case and we see a few regulars here, from time to time," WORD replied.

"So, almost 30 years without a drink. How does it seem?" THOUGHT asked.

"What d'ya think? It's like old times, like I never stopped. I can't quite put my finger on it, but it seems strangely different," Kyle said, excitedly. The faint echo of Dr. Angle lingered in his mind.

"Obviously, anyone who lays off for that long doesn't have problem?" WORD said.

"Yeah, right!" Kyle smiled.

Then he was overcome with the other voices again.

"Bernese, see if you can get Dr. Norris up here pronto," Dr. Angle said, "and get the crash-cart and standby." A moment later, "His pressure is 199 over 100; He's seizing!"

Kyle was twitching and shaking wildly.

Bernese, Lorazepam, 4 mg, IV bolus!" as Dr. Angle checked Kyle's pulse.

Bernese rushed to Kyle's side with a syringe and inserted the needle into his IV line.

"Make sure to put that in the chart, Bernese," Dr. Angle said.

Dr. Norris arrived. "Hi Dick, looks like you've got a live one here."

"Yeah, Brad, I just wanted to check with you, if there's anything else you're aware of that would have contra-indicated our standard treatment," Dr. Angle said.

"No, Dick, standard protocol is fine. According to his sister, he was heavily into alcohol at one time and was hospitalized for a serious suicide episode; damn near died according to an old chart, released from North East General, that I just received. Diagnosed with intense suicidal ideation at that time. Although that was greatly relieved after a three-month voluntary commitment. The chart also notes an earlier childhood diagnosis of Social (Pragmatic) Communication Disorder[2]. However, anecdotal family history, related by his sister, Molly, in a second meeting, adds some elements that I believe may impinge heavily on this case and in the light of this information, I must admit I'm greatly concerned as to the outcome," Dr. Norris said.

"How so?" Dr. Angle asked.

"We know his mother was hospitalized twice for serious psychotic breaks, manifesting in the form of both auditory and visual hallucinations. Kyle's sister related that the diagnosis at the time was some form of schizophrenia, although from the anecdotal information it seems more likely that a contemporary diagnosis would be manic depressive psychosis or bipolar psychosis. "

"Kyle's mother was young, under financial strain and isolated from her birth family. Kyle was four and a half when she had her first break. Having formed an unusually strong bond with his mother prior to this episode, he was severely impacted by her hospitalization; and, assuming some responsibility for this, he was subsequently very conflicted and developed severe childhood anxiety, which he masked with a fare degree of success. This of course continued to impact Kyle on into adolescence, and he had a very difficult early adulthood, according to his sister," Dr. Norris concluded.

Kyle, hearing all this, thought, "Thanks, Doc. Jesus, it isn't bad enough that I have listen to all this shit again, but it's just great the way you're spreading it around. Christ, if I ever come out of this I'll never be able to show my face again!"

---

[2]   A bona fide psychiatric condition listed in the 2013 edition of the Diagnostic and Statistical Manual of Mental Disorders (DSM -5)

He thought about what the doctor had said, and then, remembering the time when his third-grade class was taking a field trip to a historical village. He wouldn't go, because he was afraid, not knowing, *afraid of what or why*, at the time. But then, adding insult to injury, he later overheard his aunt on the phone telling his teacher he couldn't go because he would get homesick! He had cried loudly and felt so humiliated. His aunt, having become the family matriarch, meant well, but she had a terrible habit of undermining him, and he thought of several other episodes where he had also felt destroyed.

Dr. Norris went on, "Although his mother's history, in itself, would be of concern and offer abundant information in support of a productive, therapeutic, clinical relationship, it is not the greatest reason for my concerns regarding a satisfactory outcome in this case."

"Oh?" Dr. Angle said, raising an eyebrow.

"Again, according to Kyle's sister, their father also suffered a painful past. He had lost his own father as a young boy of 10. Several years later he came home to discover his mother had hung herself. This episode, understandably, followed Kyle's father the rest of his life."

"In the maturation process the father managed to suppress the tremendous impact this had on him. Although he graduated from the state agricultural college, the incident stunted his development and affected him psychologically for the rest of his life. He had a lower-level career as a herdsman on the dairy farm of a state hospital. My concern for Kyle stems from his father's history of epileptic seizures of unknown etiology. To the best of his sister's recollection, clinicians were unable to identify any organic or psychopathology for two episodes that occurred in his life, separated by approximately 15 years."

"The best explanation given at the time of the second episode was that his body was reacting to significant internal mental conflict, manifesting in the form of a grand mal seizure, of idiopathic nature, and followed by an extended postictal state, or coma, of several weeks' duration. After each episode, the father seemed to have recovered enough to project a functional self-image. But after the last episode his mental health deteriorated to a point where he manifested severe overt anxiety and exhibited paranoid thinking and behavior and was treated with ECT that had an immediate positive effect and relieved his immediate symptoms. However, he soon deteriorated, again exhibiting anxiety and paranoid thinking, and was subsequently moved to a long-term-care facility where he lived out his remaining years."

"Summing up my concerns, which, of course, I must do in the absence of a psychiatric profile of Kyle, while he is suffering from a TBI, is certainly difficult. But I believe that, not unlike his father, Kyle has now suffered a grand mal seizure, idiopathic in nature, and he likely will remain in an extended postictal state or coma."

"Apparently, upon this recent admission he was nonreactive, but he is now exhibiting some form of psychic distress of an unknown nature. Given that his sister related that he did a significant amount psychotherapy earlier in his life that seemed to relieve his bouts of drinking and self-defeating behaviors, I do speculate that this seizure may have been brought on by internal stress, as the product of being in a dreamlike state, perhaps confronting something like a significant nightmare as the precipitating factor."

"I am hopeful that it is merely dream-work that is taking place, but I also remain guarded and worry that this man may degenerate into a vegetative state or that he will regain consciousness in a demented form," Dr. Norris concluded.

Kyle, dumbfounded at this recounted history, thought, "God damn, Doc, certainly a sobering moment." He chuckled to himself. "Boy, when you say it like that, I sure don't like the odds." Then he thought, "Jesus, poor Dad, if ever there was a tragic life, and the hell of it was he lived through almost every damned moment of it, except when he was out of it. I wonder if he got wrapped up in letters and words then too. Worst yet, I sure as hell hope I make out better than he did. Christ, give me a break!" Kyle thought, subdued, dumbfounded and totally blank.

"Wow, Brad, thanks. What a history. This guy surely deserves a break and it's a bit overwhelming too. Talk about hereditary predisposition, this really takes the cake," Dr. Angle said.

"No problem Dick, but please keep me posted and please have Bernese put a note in his record to notify me if anything crops up and you're not around," Dr. Norris said, when leaving.

Bernese, having been standing by as Dr. Norris related this background and his guarded prognosis, asked, "Do you think he'll make it, doctor?"

"It looks pretty bleak to me, but there's always a chance, and we have to do everything on our side to give him the best chance possible," Dr. Angle said.

"Yeah, right, Doc. If all this palaver, with you and that other doctor, exposing my dirty linen, is the best you can do then I don't like the odds much either," Kyle thought, as Bernese and the doctor walked away.

In the silence, Kyle found himself back at Slattery's, sitting with THOUGHT and WORD, but he felt strange and unusually awkward.

"Jesus, you've got something that sounds pretty bad'" WORD said.

"You heard?" Kyle asked.

"Yeah, both of us," THOUGHT said, "You look different too!"

Looking down at himself, Kyle shrieked, "What's happened, oh, my God, I'm totally different! What am I? What am I going to do?"

"You look like a REPROBATE," WORD replied, "That's not really as bad as it sounds. You're just hung by your own petard, and presto. In the Land of Words, you are what you make yourself out to be. All that talk about your drinking, so what did you expect?"

"What a hell of a thing, I had no idea!" Kyle said hysterically. "Jesus, I could be stuck here forever with you guys!"

He jumped up, ran over to the mirror behind the bar and screamed, "Oh My God!"

Looking back at him was a smartly dressed creature with horns pointing through the brim of a stovepipe hat, accented by a black swallowtail coat. It was almost more than he could take. "A devil emoji!" he yelled.

"That guy Brad really put it out there. Don't you think, THOUGHT?" WORD said, laughing.

"Yeah, what the hell does he know? Don't worry, Kyle, we'll kick you out when you're ready," THOUGHT said.

"That's supposed to make me feel better!"

"Yeah it is," WORD said, looking at Kyle. "So, tell us about it."

"Wait just a minute. Is this some kind of test or something? How will I know, what do I have to do to get out of here?" Kyle pleaded.

"Dreams have a way of abating and look, your old man got out, so bide your time and let's get on with it," WORD said.

"Yeah, let's hear it from your side," THOUGHT said.

"You guys sure aren't very convincing, but okay. God, maybe I'll have some kind of metamorphosis and become a word for ever. What a thought!," he mused. "First I 'll have another Bud though," he said, catching the bartender's eye.

Then he continued on, while sipping the fresh full glass with a frothy head, "I used to think if you had my problems you'd drink too. Now I know better. Even so, I'm back in it, and just remember, you guys asked for it. All the shit that comes down is on you two!"

"First though, all that clinical stuff is mostly bullshit. My mom and dad were the kindest and most loving people and either one would give you the shirt off their back. I loved my Mom very deeply. She was a voracious reader. You name it; she read it. She absolutely loved music and had a profound richness of spirit. But she was terribly shy and ever after her nervous breakdowns, she was always somewhat detached from reality in all matters to do with religion; her belief in God was profound and unshakeable! She even claimed one of her ears was circumcised in a covenant with God, as an act of purification! Of course, as a young boy, I was alarmed by such outlandish claims and didn't understand when she went off on one these religious tangents. Sometimes I'd feel embarrassed when she acted oddly in front of friends, but I never let that show because I loved her so much."

"My dad was also gentle, a shy sort too. He read far and wide also, but was more a sampler than a deep reader like mom. He did have an incredible knowledge and a way with animals. They both especially loved flowers, vegetable and flower gardens and all things of the natural world. When they were younger they would take long walks in the woods. These are all the wonderful things that I inherited, in spite of these damn doctors' *hereditary predisposition*," Kyle said, mockingly.

"We know there's lots of good there, but you are carrying a little baggage. Don't you think?" WORD said.

"Amen to that," THOUGHT added.

Kyle, by then feeling the pops, blurted out, "You guys don't know the half of it. Shouldn't the saying be 'every silver lining has a dark cloud lurking' – or something like that."

Having just extolled his father's virtues, he thought back to just before his teenage years, when he was ashamed of his father and often worried that he was going to grow up to be just like him.

He had seen his father then as afraid of everything and not very able to stand up for himself. Now he thought it strange that he so quickly and without reservation had spoken of him in such glowing terms.

Picking up with his conversation, "God, I have changed. In spite of myself, I'm more like my father than I realized. Anyway, of course, with the inherited emotional baggage in the background, I was shy, scared of other people, and terrified of making mistakes, so for years I was held captive by feelings of insecurity and low self-esteem. I clowned around in school and I generally amounted to nothing. In high school, I discovered the magic elixir, John Barleycorn, and cutting to the chase, I became a garden-variety drunk!"

"That's it, that's your explanation?" WORD asked, a twinge of disgust in his voice.

Kyle, sometimes slurring his words, "Of course not, but how long do you have?"

"Whatever it takes," WORD replied.

"Okay, okay! Christ, I joined the military, and after a year and a half, I tried to kill myself and was mustered out on a medical discharge with enough personal shame to sink a ship. It became a deep secret that I tried to ignore by pouring booze on the wound, but there was no escaping and another serious suicide attempt landed me in a psychiatric hospital. I wish I could say they waved a magic wand over me and poof I was restored, but a recovery of a different sort was extended, psychotherapy, you know, the luxury of the rich. Anyway, the therapist was a wonderful man who took me on a long journey of self-discovery, and on to a professional education and career," Kyle said, stopping short.

"Go on," THOUGHT said.

"Nah, you'd think that would be enough and I'd be cured, but John Barleycorn makes a tough bargain, as you can now see. God, my being here at Slattery's again is a nightmare. It just doesn't seem quite real, maybe a 'drunk-dream'," Kyle moaned.

"Yeah, it really is a nightmare, but you'll get through it. We've got all the time in the world," WORD said.

"That's what I'm afraid of," Kyle replied, but realizing that his mind had eased in a kind of catharsis. Through sharing part of his life's story, he felt relieved and more like his former self.

Other voices were intruding again.

"He's stabilized and I think he should rest well tonight. Tell the night shift to keep a close eye on him. They'll be coming in any minute. He can't afford many of these seizure events; they tend to cook the brain," Dr. Angle said, walking off.

"Jesus, did you hear that?" Kyle said.

"Yeah, but don't worry, they don't have all the answers. That's enough for today. You're coming home with me," WORD said, adding, "Come on, drink up and let's get going. A good night's rest and you'll feel a lot better about all this."

"Oh, God, yes, you'll get no argument from me," Kyle replied, and, sure enough, his former image reappeared in the mirror. They left Slattery's and walked the short distance to WORD'S home.

"Welcome, welcome," WORD said, in the front entryway and then calling to his wife, ETYMOLOGY, "Honey, I'm home. We have a guest."

"Hi darling," came from a hallway nearby, and then Mrs. WORD came out, her raven black hair on the shoulders of her rather square body, that looked like a large dictionary with a picture of WORD on front. Smiling, she reached out her hand to Kyle, while asking WORD, "Who is this handsome I?"

"He's a new friend and prefers to be called Kyle."

"Oh, Kyle, let me see, yes from the Scottish surname, of course. Nice to meet you," ETYMOLOGY said as she shook Kyle's hand. "And to what do we owe this visit?" she asked.

WORD, replied, "We've just been over at Slattery's with THOUGHT, and Kyle's a little tired, so I thought it made sense for him to come here. He's new to the area, it's late and I didn't want him getting lost."

"That place again; honey, can't you find a better place to take your guests?" Turning to Kyle she said, "You're more than welcome, Kyle. How about a cup of nice warm cocoa before bed?"

"Thank you, but I don't think so. I'd really like to lie down," Kyle said, noticing that as she shifted positions the picture of WORD on her front changed, showing WORD in various poses.

"How weird, too much to drink," Kyle thought.

"Make yourself at home, but please ignore the décor. We're hoping to redecorate this year," she said, directing Kyle to the guest quarters, down a hallway from the kitchen. "Please be careful not to mistake it for the Nursery next door. There are a lot of little toddlers in there that I've just put down."

"Really, you have some small children?" Kyle asked.

"Every year," she said, winking at WORD, "About 300 this year! God, I don't know how I manage. WORD, you really have to step-up this year. I don't know why, but this year they're more than a handful!"

As Kyle shuffled down to his room he noticed everything was decorated with words. The wall coverings were comprised of words and phrases in different colors. Even the lamps, when he looked carefully, were elongated or stretched out words or letters in some form or other.

"How strange, sleep?" Kyle thought as he entered the room and climbed into bed, only to be amazed as he realized, there was Betsy in her nighty and looking all welcoming. Then just as he was embracing her and feeling so aroused, there was a knock on the door. "Damnit," Kyle exclaimed as he left Betsy lying there, got up, opened the door, and there to his utter surprise was WORD. "What is it now? Can't you see I'm busy?" But then to his further distress, as he looked over his shoulder back towards the bed, Betsy was gone.

"Come on, it's time to get going," WORD said. "You don't want to sleep your life away, do you?"

"What are you talking about, Jesus Christ, I just barely got here!"

"Well, sometimes it just seems that way. I know you were really tired. Let's get going," WORD replied, adding, "We're going to tour the town."

A WORD ABOUT TOWN

"So where are we headed?" Kyle asked.

"This way, out the back door. We're heading into town." WORD said, then looking at Kyle, "What is it now? You look so glum."

"Oh, nothing, just crazy dreams, I guess." Then thinking to himself, "Jesus, for a long time it seemed like every time I got close to a woman, something got in the way and I never got to carry it off." He thought of Pauline, a high school sweetheart, and the time he parked with her one night and they were smooching it up, but he just couldn't bring himself to even begin to have sex with her. He was confused and humiliated after dropping her off. "She was so beautiful, what the hell was wrong with me?" Then his mood changed as he thought of Betsy, "She's great," he thought, "No problems there, the shrink and growing up took care of that issue," he thought, feeling relieved.

Perking up, Kyle realized they were back in the library, but again the stacks were mysteriously streets, crowded with other words, moving in one direction or another. A background noise like that of any busy town. The sounds as words passed by and noise caused by the general hustle and bustle of urban life surrounded them. But without dwelling on this, Kyle's attention was focused on the appearances in the different parts of the town. Some sections were filled with beautiful houses that looked like books and that had titles on them of the great literary masterpieces, while other sections were filled with books whose titles were fairy-tales or romances. One part of the town was really packed with volumes whose titles or names Kyle had never heard of, but he thought they generated a very dirty atmosphere. The industrial section was filled with books that had inscriptions on them of a rather technical nature.

Finally, they walked onto a main thoroughfare where there were all sorts of public institutions and stores, all with the appearance of different books.

Kyle was studying a structure across the street from where they were standing. The inscription on the front of it read, **QUEENSBERRY RULES**. "That's a rather odd name. What is it?"

"Oh, that's the courthouse. Let's go over; I think a trial should be starting in a little while. Trials are always interesting," WORD replied.

After crossing the street and entering, WORD led Kyle down a maze of corridors and into a large room. Going to the front of the room they took seats as close to the front as a spoked banister allowed. The clatter of chairs moving, opening and closing of doors added an air of mystery and suspense. Shortly the room was filled, but the area beyond the banister, in front of Kyle and THOUGHT, where words, obviously officials because of their attire, were setting up the defense and prosecutor's tables, placing microphones, adding water pitchers with glasses and spare writing tablets.

Very quickly, after the front area became settled, a clamor in the back of the courtroom attracted everyone's attention towards two officious guards who were escorting a word, obviously the defendant, towards the front of the court. He looked like a set of balance scales that kept disappearing from view.

Everyone in the court was craning their necks to get a look at the defendant, but it was very difficult to see him unless the light was just right!

After the defendant was seated, the court clerk, the perfect resemblance of a monkey-wrench, in official attire, stepped forward and began speaking: "Hear ye, hear ye. All rise. The court in and for the realm of **Queensberry**, the honorable judge, MANIPULATE, presiding, is now in session."

The judge, from all appearances a multipurpose tool, with official robes and wearing a gray wig, mumbled, "Be seated."

Again, the clerk stepped to the fore and began reading a document, with a big red seal, "Case number 249 of the court of **Queensberry** versus the defendant, JUSTICE. The charge against the defendant being stated thusly: That you, JUSTICE, have with malicious intent deceived the world; that is, that you have caused yourself to look like something which you are not, and that you have led people to believe that you are perfect when you are not, that you have led a life of deceit and that, in fact, although you are a word of some meaning, you have passed yourself off as representing equity, impartiality, and fair-play." Turning towards the judge, he continued, "Let the record show that the charges against the defendant have been stated. The court with his honor's permission is ready to hear the case." The clerk then seated himself.

The judge said, "The court will hear opening statements."

The prosecutor, who looked like a sword, stood and walked to the front of the court. He then turned and, facing the court, said, "We, that is, the citizens of Queensberry, intend to prove, beyond a shadow of a doubt, that the defendant, JUSTICE, has fraudulently and willfully acted in a manner so as to take on a different appearance in the eyes of others. That being to look like one of righteousness, fair-play, equity, impartiality, etc. We further contend that no one word can incorporate or even aspire to incorporate a composite of such ideology. Our proof shall be that by the very absence of this ideology in anyone of a number of instances conclusively proves that JUSTICE does not exist, as the defendant would have us believe. For if such a purported thing were to exist, the intolerable conditions which attest to its absence could not themselves exist to bear such testimony." Then, turning towards the judge, he continued, "That is all the prosecution has to say at this time, your Honor." The prosecutor took his chair.

The judge nodded to the defense attorney, an indication for him to make his opening statement.

The counselor, in the form of a shield, took his position, where his counterpart had previously stood, and began, "It is by the very nature of this congregation that the defendant, JUSTICE, can exist. Should you, the jury, find him guilty of the allegations that our noble prosecutor alleges you will have undermined the very pillars upon which this revered court stands. Without the existence of the defendant, no trial can aspire to be fair. It is often only in instances and places such as this that the defendant can exist. Thus, a finding against him is in essence a finding against this court. We contend that a guilty verdict can only be one of injustice, that being a trial absent of all the qualities my client stands for. However, it is the wish of my client to prove his existence in the same manner as the prosecutor intends to disprove it. He believes that if he, JUSTICE, is to be, then no certain amount of logic or semantics can disprove that which is. For if it can do so then it certainly does not exist." Turning toward the judge, "That is all, your Honor." He took his chair.

The judge, turning towards the jury, a hodgepodge of different words, said, "I urge you to seek the truth and to discharge your duty accordingly."

Then, turning towards the prosecutor, he stated, "The prosecution may begin."

The prosecutor stood, saying, "Your Honor, I call our first witness."

The image of a torch stepped forward, casting a beautiful white light over his immediate vicinity.

The clerk stepped in front of the torch, a very illuminating picture, to be sure, and, holding out in his left hand the *Holy Bible*, said, "Place your left hand upon this book and raise your right hand."

The torch did so.

The Clerk continued, "Do you swear to tell the whole truth and nothing but the truth, so help you God?"

Before the torch could answer, the counselor jumped up yelling, "Objection! Objection! Your Honor."

"And to what does counsel object?" asked the judge.

"Surely, holding one's hand on some book and swearing before any number of deities is no prerequisite for truth," said the counselor.

"I remind the counselor that this is established courtroom procedure, a tradition if you please," the judge said.

"Your Honor, if my client is to have a fair trial we cannot stand on tradition. We object because my client and I find no credit in such a charade, a condition that we feel is not so likely to be found in the minds of the jury. We say let the truth of the witness be borne in his statements themselves. Have not countless perjurers sworn to similar oaths?"

"Overruled!" replied the judge, banging his gavel, "The witness will answer the question."

"I do," said the torch.

"Be seated," said the clerk.

The prosecutor stepped forward and asked of the witness, "Please state you name and profession?"

"Objection, Objection!" yelled the counselor. "Your Honor, this line of questioning is immaterial. We care only to hear what the witness has to say. Certainly, his name and profession can serve only to give credit or discredit to his testimony, a condition hardly suitable to a fair trial. We cannot accept this line of questioning unless it be to establish an expert witness."

"Overruled!" replied the judge. With a banging of his gavel, he continued, "The witness will state his name and occupation."

"I am TRUTH, the whole TRUTH, and nothing but TRUTH," said the witness.

"Objection!" yelled the counselor, "Your Honor, we demand to know the credibility of this witness. I submit the witness has just perjured himself."

Turning towards the witness, the counselor continued. "The witness claims to be nothing but TRUTH; are you not, in fact, a word of some substance?"

The prosecutor looked flabbergasted.

The witness just smiled and replied, "I am indeed that which you say and conversely that very word is the TRUTH. I make no attempt to put anyone on, nor to take anyone off. I represent a state of being, a testament of only that which was or was not, is or is not, is about to be or not about to be."

A noisy undercurrent of chatter and murmurs welled up in the courtroom.

"Order in the court," called the judge. "The objection is sustained; the prosecutor shall establish the credibility of the witness."

The prosecutor walked over to his table and picked up a document bearing a big blue seal and the words **Birth Certificate**. The prosecutor, holding it up before the court, said, "Your Honor, we enter citizen's exhibit number 1, which states that the witness came into being with the first man and woman."

The counselor stood up saying, "Your Honor, we do not question the validity of the document. However, the document does not say that this witness came into being at that moment, but only that TRUTH did. I further submit, your Honor, that there is no one present who can attest to the identity of the witness. It is only the fear of jeopardizing their own creditability that has kept members of this court from singling out the witness as blatant fraud. I would ask is there anyone present who can so identify the witness as TRUTH?"

JUSTICE jumped up crying, "Fools! All of you are fools. Whosoever of you can know the truth? You can only know a part of the truth; namely, it is a partial truth that no one present can identify the witness. I would rest easily if it were not so. Your failure to recognize me for what I am is as much a part truth. Should we all see the witness in his true light my existence would not be in question."

"Well said," cried the witness. "To know the whole truth about a given thing is to know all that there is to know about it, and to know all that, one must know what one does not know; and since one can never know what one does not know, one can only know part truths or that part of the truth that one knows. If, however, the court will accept my testimony as only that of a word of some substance, I believe I can shed some light on the matter at hand."

The judge ordered, "The counselor and prosecutor will approach the bench."

Kyle, consumed by all the theatrics, thought back to the time he was arrested for a DUI, after a bad auto accident. He had been completely drunk and had no business driving. At the scene of the accident, first he agreed to take a breathalyzer, but then refused, thinking about his rights, because if he had failed the test it would have meant an automatic suspension of his license. But once sober and in court, he was full of remorse and pleaded guilty to the DUI charge and subsequently lost his license for over a year!

He turned to WORD saying, "I had to go to court once and was found guilty for driving under the influence. Of course, I continued right on drinking, but there sure as hell wasn't any of this folderol in that court."

"I think there's just a little more at stake here," WORD replied.

"Yeah, justice, that's pretty important stuff! I've often wondered if there really is anything like real justice anyway. Seems like no one is ever satisfied with decisions that courts make," Kyle said. "I wish the judge had thrown the book at me. You know given me something to think about; maybe forced me to go to treatment or get involved in a 12-step program."

"There you go, finding someone else to fix your problems -- if only the judge had sent you to treatment all your problems would be solved. Come-on, own it, take responsibility and get involved in fixing yourself. After all, justice at its best, is still a mixed bag. If you're looking for perfection you've come to the wrong place," WORD said.

"I'm not exactly here by choice," Kyle said, a little piqued.

"Shush, they're getting ready to start up again," WORD replied.

After the short conference with the judge, the two attorneys went back to their respective tables and the judge ordered, "A motion to waive positive identification of the witness has been sustained. The jury will disregard all testimony and evidence that indicated the witness is TRUTH. The prosecution may continue."

The Prosecutor said to the witness, "Please continue."

TRUTH said, "No doubt everyone here has heard the phrase, 'the truth will out.' I can't count the number of times when the truth did come to light but too late for justice to manifest itself. This brings to mind a recent case of a young woman with terminal cancer, who fought long and hard for a euthanasia law to be passed in the great state of California. In time the legislature and state Governor managed to pass the bill into law, but with a delayed implementation to take place in the following year. The young woman died six months before implementation. Yes, the young woman did help to get a law passed that would give dignity to the terminally ill, but it was too late for her and she suffered a horribly painful death."

The prosecutor asked, "Wouldn't you call this a case of injustice?"

"It depends on how you look at it," TRUTH replied. "Certainly, there is justice for those for whom the law will apply when it is fully enacted, but for the young woman the only justice, if at all, was that she knew she was successful in her efforts in getting the law passed, very little comfort on her death-bed I'm sure!"

"But isn't this a rather trivial example, of justice versus injustice, in the larger scheme of the world and the horrible things that take place?" the prosecutor asked.

"Yes, I guess you could say so," TRUTH replied, "but, as you know, justice is blind and it certainly is a subjective thing, at best. Oh, there are countless instances of horrible injustices that have occurred. The fact that over six million innocent Jews were killed in the Nazi pogrom of WWII is a good example, of such injustice. However, it doesn't mean that no justice came out of that horrendous atrocity. After all, the war was won by the Allies and the Jews now have their own state of Israel," said TRUTH.

"But isn't that just it; there was no justice for those six million Jews, only heinous injustice." Then, turning to the jury, the prosecutor said, "Ladies and Gentlemen, I submit if justice exists at all, then where was it when these terrible things were going on? Can we really assume any measure of justice for all those victims, just because the allies won the war and the state of Israel was formed?" Then, turning toward the counselor, the prosecutor said, "Your Witness."

The counselor approaching the witness asked, "Since you allege to be TRUTH, how do you see it; was there any real justice for the young woman, or, for that matter, the six million Jews?"

TRUTH replied, "Justice has no choice where it is applied. In many cases, it doesn't exist at all and in most other cases, only partial justice holds sway. Only in a small number of situations does full justice prevail. There is almost always some element of injustice that survives in the affairs of the world."

The counselor then asked, "Must we then conclude that justice doesn't exist at all, if it doesn't exist in every case, or, at the least, manifest itself at some level in every case or situation? Are we to conclude that justice can't coexist in the presence of injustice?"

"No," TRUTH replied, "justice can always exist, in any place, at any time, when it is brought into practice and fully applied."

At this moment, a clamor broke out in the back of the court. A strange figure, appearing like a broken scale one moment and then looking like the defendant JUSTICE the next moment, was muscling his way towards the front of the court and nothing, including the guards, seemed to be able to stop him.

Kyle asked, WORD who this was.

"Oh, that's INJUSTICE," WORD replied.

"I don't understand," Kyle said. "He looks just like JUSTICE one moment and then something quite different the next."

"Yes," WORD replied. "He's a parasite; he hangs on JUSTICE'S coattails and tries really hard to remain totally transparent, but he just can't pull it off here where JUSTICE is under such scrutiny. In every case and situation where JUSTICE is present, INJUSTICE abides; though often unseen and unnoticed, he's just waiting to pounce at the first opportunity."

Just then the judge ordered, "Court officers, remove this object from the court!"

The officers moved quickly trying to corral the unruly object and when it looked like they finally had him in custody, he slipped from their grasp and just disappeared.

The counselor jumped up from his chair and, looking at the judge, he yelled. "Objection, your Honor! We call for a mistrial. How can a trial with INJUSTICE present, even with the hint of him, be fair; that's bound to prejudice the jury?"

At this the prosecutor jumped up yelling, "Your Honor, INJUSTICE has been removed from the court. We beg your Honor's indulgence to let the trial proceed."

The judge banged his gavel and said, "I'm ordering a mistrial! JUSTICE, if it is to exist at all, must be preserved at all costs. I cannot let it appear to those who leave this court that they might mistake INJUSTICE for JUSTICE. As it stands, we all have a different idea of what JUSTICE looks like and in almost all cases there are some who will see INJUSTICE at the end of most trials, so here, above all, we must act 'in the interest of JUSTICE' to insure these proceedings are just and totally fair!"

At this the prosecutor called, "Your Honor, is it not just as much a miscarriage of justice to declare a mistrial?"

"No," replied the judge. "If we are to err it must always be in favor of the defendant."

The counselor jumped up saying, "Your Honor, we commend your decision, and, I would add, JUSTICE was served here today! Our position is that real justice, like beauty, is in the eye or mind of the beholder and subsequently there is always dissent at every finding, with some or many, as the case may be, believing one or the other prevailed. Even now there are those who believe there was not justice here today, but I can tell you he is alive and well, but it is only in the guise of justice that injustice so often prevails."

"The court is adjourned," came with a banging of the gavel.

"I don't understand. Everybody knows there's very little that's fair in this world," Kyle said.

"How long have you been here? Semantics, that's the name of the game here. After all, nuances are a word's bread and butter—our *raison d'être!*" WORD concluded, adding, "Lets' get going."

As Kyle and WORD worked their way through the clamor of spectators leaving the courthouse, they ran into THOUGHT, who said hello to Kyle and then, without waiting for Kyle's reply, he turned to WORD and pointing to Kyle said, "How's he doing, is he catching on at all?"

"He's a slow learner, I'm afraid," WORD replied. "I think some remedial training should be the order of the day."

"That's easily arranged," THOUGHT replied. The Academy is nearby. Why don't we both take him?"

"Wait just a minute, you guys; here I am at a pivotal moment and you two just want to go on as though nothing happened. When we came out today, I thought it would be a little excursion around town and a chance to forget my troubles for awhile. I had no idea we would get caught up in a philosophical juggernaut on justice and truth," Kyle was whining again.

"Further, after that last episode at Slattery's, I feel like I'm trapped. The Docs can't seem to help, other than to provide custodial care in hopes that someday I'll wake up. And this place, with you guys, what the hell, I'm scared to death that I'll never wake up and get out of here!"

"Yeah, maybe we've been pushing a bit hard," WORD said.

"I just don't know, except that I feel like I have some unresolved issues that I have to clear up, and I feel so conflicted and all stirred up inside, like I'm never going to get out of here unless they're resolved or something. After what the Docs said about dream-work and my prognosis, I'm thinkin' it could all be on me," Kyle replied.

"I had planned on some remedial study for you at the Academy, and I still think that might be best, but we'll bear in mind your personal concerns and we can all see where that takes you," THOUGHT said, leading the three of them from the courthouse.

REMEDIAL STUDIES

"Here we are," THOUGHT said.

They were standing at the front gate to a large complex that reminded Kyle of his undergraduate campus, except strange objects were walking and moving about much like students and faculty on any campus.

Through the gate he could see a large open space surrounded on three sides by buildings that also harkened back to Kyle's undergraduate days, and at this moment a marching band looked to be practicing a typical march. "Wow, this is it, my old campus, with the band on the Quad and all." Then seeing the inscription at the top of the gate, *ACADEMY OF ADVANCED LEARNING*, he frowned, "What are you guys up to now?" he asked.

"It's time you got a real education!" WORD replied. "It's back to school for you."

"School, what are you talking about? I've already been to all the schools I need. After all I did graduate magna cum laude!"

"That means nothing here." Turning to THOUGHT, WORD continued, "You tell him!"

"You need to start all over if you're going to make it here. First it will be grammar school for you, but before that you have to get indoctrinated."

"What are you talking about?" Kyle demanded, in a very exasperated tone. "You guys are too much. Why not just start in kindergarten; really, give me a break and stop messing with me!"

"We're not kidding. When we say grammar school that's just what we mean, literally, with the emphasis on grammar! How do you expect to get on in the Land of Words when you don't know the proper etiquette?"

"Get off it! I do know how to speak!" Kyle said angrily.

"No, you just think you do, but here it's important that you address other words in the right manner or you'll shortly learn you're a pariah and you'll find yourself back in Limbo, where you came from in the first place."

"Limbo, where, what are you talking about?" Kyle stammered.

"You know, when you were first in the hospital and you couldn't talk with anyone in the hospital and we came to your rescue. That couldn't have been very pleasant. Then in the Land of Letters you kept going on about spelling and grammar as the bane of your existence. Well here we are – a chance to start over."

Kyle was angry, perceiving this as manipulation, but he felt captured, vulnerable, and didn't want to rock the boat, so he remained passive as WORD and THOUGHT dragged him off to a nineteenth-century, admissions building and the Registrar's office, that also stirred Kyle's memory.

"What's he here for?" an object, looking like an academic mace, with dark brown hair and a full-length plain dress, asked.

"Oh my God, it's her, the old battleax herself!" Kyle hissed, and as he looked at this figure his mind flashed back to his college years and the Registrar who tried to deny him credit for courses he was applying to have put on his academic transcript. "Next thing you know students will be expecting credit for Dale Carnegie, courses," she had told him, denying his application!

"You're going to give me those credits, lady, or you're going to find yourself down in the local court house!" He had yelled back. He had then gone to the head dean to contest her decision and felt totally vindicated when the dean overruled the registrar, and he was given credit! But now he realized he had unwittingly harbored a grudge against her all that time.

"God, resentments eat you up piecemeal," he thought.

WORD stepped up saying, "He's here for Introduction to Grammar and Library Initiation."

"He looks like a difficult case. Are you sure he's up to it? He reminds me of someone from long ago who was a real instigator," the Registrar remarked, as she pushed her chair back and stepped forward confronting them all.

"You don't know the half of it!" THOUGHT replied.

"Now wait just a minute, I'm fully qualified and I have a master's degree to prove it," Kyle angrily interjected. At this point he was blushing from total embarrassment, not to mention a good degree of anger. "What's wrong with you two, this place is crazy! I'm perfectly fine the way I am," he retorted, angrily.

"Looks like he is qualified at entry level," the Registrar said, dismissively handing a certificate to Kyle, who thought back to his undergraduate years when he had started with an emphasis on psychology, thinking of a possible career, but the entry level courses were so pedestrian that he had switched and had become an English major! Now in this place, these two wanting him to start all over, "What the hell!" he thought, also accepting the fact that a degree in English Lit doesn't guarantee competence in spelling and grammar. He now realized he was living proof of that!

"See that wasn't so bad. We don't want to just abandon you and leave you to your own devices. I'm sure you remember how well you did after crossing The Bridge?" THOUGHT said.

"Okay, okay, I'll play along for now, but you two better know what you're doing," Kyle said grudgingly.

"Well, let's run him over to the Library," WORD said to THOUGHT.

"Starting at the library; Jesus, I guess we just start from scratch," Kyle thought, feeling despondent.

It was beautiful sunny day as the three companions started walking, the band was still playing and had just struck up *The Washington Post* March. For some reason Kyle felt at home as he stepped out in front and started walking, weaving amongst other objects going about their daily business.

"Seems like he knows where he's going," THOUGHT said, as the three were approaching a very stately looking building, with the inscription over the entrance:

LIBRARY
REPOSITORY OF KNOWLEDGE

On entering they were confronted with an array of signs pointing in different directions and with other words running around. Except for the signs Kyle had no idea of what was what or where.

"I'm totally confused. It's not the library where I did my undergraduate research. It's oddly different from the other libraries I've known. Where's the information desk?"

Pointing to a large tree a short distance from them, "It's right over there," THOUGHT said.

"But that's not an information desk, certainly not in any proper sense. It says, *Tree of the Knowledge of Good and Evil*, so what gives?"

"Same difference," THOUGHT replied.

"Good and Evil is the same as an information desk? Give me a break, and this is what passes for a library?" Kyle turned to his two companions to remonstrate. "Now this I have to see."

"In our library world yes," WORD said. "All knowledge is equal in a divine sense. There is no good or evil knowledge of itself, only that thinking and doing makes it so."

"What do they do then with the evil ones who come to the library?" Kyle asked.

"Well some day we may do lie-detector tests, but for now we let visitors exercise 'free will', and their lives are what they make of them, good or bad," WORD said. "But then, of course, we can always look at what they're reading if we're so disposed. You know 'Big Brother' is never very far away."

As the three of them walked over to the tree, Kyle spied this thing, sitting there, that looked just like an 'eye' and at this sight Kyle immediately got a very puzzled look, saying, "Now what?"

"Oh, that's just the All-Seeing Eye, you know, the so-called Eye of Providence – God watching over us all and that sort," THOUGHT said. "Just ask for what you want."

"God!" Kyle exclaimed, "I don't know that I even believe in God!"

"Just a figure of speech," THOUGHT said. "Think of it as the commonly referenced, '**G**ood **O**rderly **D**irection,' just a symbol of whatever governs in the affairs of the world, if anything ever does."

"But, I don't know what I want," Kyle protested.

"Remedial Grammar?" THOUGHT reminded him.

"Okay, okay!" Kyle replied and walked over to the Eye, who was engaged with another patron.

The patron, who looked like a shark, said, "I'm looking for something on the great misanthropes in history, what do you suggest?"

"Believe me, sonny, there is no such thing as a great misanthrope! However, if you must persist in the pursuit of the oxymoron, try Nietzsche in conjunction with nihilism," the eye replied and continued, "Next…"

Kyle stepped forward, "What do you have on Remedial Grammar?"

"What language?" the Eye replied, raising its eyelid.

"English, of course."

"Is that Old English, Middle English or Modern English?"

"Oh, Modern."

"So, Modern English Grammar, go to the catalog in *Circulation* and look under modern languages. That's down the hallway to your left, just past *Serial Records* and up one flight of stairs," the Eye said.

Kyle turned and started walking down the hallway with THOUGHT and WORD. They hadn't gone very far at all before they saw the sign *Serial Records* and just then Kyle heard a whizzing sound and realized the air around them was filled with strange particles, almost like dust, but flying past them.

"What's all this?" Kyle asked.

"Oh, it's nothing really, just the data streaming by for the various serials indexed by the library."

All of this seemed so incongruous to Kyle, in the light of his own experience with a Master's in Library and Information Science, no less. "Please," he protested, "you aren't really trying to tell me these are the magazines and journals that I deal with so frequently?"

"That's right," THOUGHT replied.

Just when Kyle thought he could no longer tell where he was going, because of the clouds of data flying by, they reached the stairs and the air became clear again. At the top of the stairs, and to the right, they entered a large room with a sign, *Circulation*, over the doorway. As they entered, Kyle couldn't really see any end to the room. There were several rows of computer terminals and then filing cabinets that succeeded one after another off into the distance, and again with no end in sight. Patrons of all colors and stripes were engaged at various cabinets and at some of the computers. The room was humming with a light undercurrent of background noise.

Kyle turned to Word saying, "I'm confused, what do I do now? I just want to look up a book! Where in God's name do I begin? What's with all these cabinets, anyway?"

"You sure have a lot of questions. You can either use the computer or look it up the old way in the Card-Catalog."

"Wow, that's a Card-Catalog? I thought they went out with the inquisition."

"**The** Card-Catalog," THOUGHT interjected.

"I think I'll try that, I'd like to see how they do it here."

With that, Kyle turned to the Card-Catalog and started down the first aisle of the A's which continued into the second aisle and on into the third aisle, before he gave up and turning to WORD he said, "What is going on, where are the B's or the C's, etc.?"

"Oh, they're out there somewhere," WORD replied.

"What do you mean, somewhere?" Isn't there any end to this?"

"No! There isn't! What do you expect? This library holds all the knowledge there is, both good and evil, it goes on and on and on and on... Let's just say, you'll be quite a while before you get to the G's or R's. It just might be easier if you try the computer."

With that Kyle turned and went back to the computers and, as he stepped up to one, it turned on as he approached. As he touched the keyboard, the Eye appeared on the screen.

"What are you looking for?"

"God, it's you again. Don't you remember, I'm looking for English grammar?"

"What do you think, you're the only one that comes here? I have infinite patrons from everywhere, and I'm supposed to remember every question?" the Eye replied. "You must be pretty damn self-centered. Now, what is it you want?"

"Remedial Grammar."

"You could just say Modern English Grammar," the Eye replied.

"I thought you didn't remember my question."

"I didn't say, I don't remember, but that's not my job and just maybe you changed your mind in the interim. And just in case you missed it, the world isn't all about you, you know. Besides I thought you were here for remedial study. Obviously, you haven't learned anything! Now, let me see," the Eye mused, "That will be in aisle number 7,285,000,027."

"My God!" cried Kyle, "how on earth am I supposed to get there and find that?"

"Go back out into the hall where you came in and go to the elevators on the left and punch in the number and the elevator will take you to that area. Let me warn you before you start, no funny business in the stacks. I'll be watching."

"Who, what, do you think I am, a hood or criminal?" Kyle protested.

"For all I know you might be a bookworm or some new form of mold in disguise," the Eye replied. "Besides, even those who intend to do no harm are forever doing something that upsets the order of things, taking books off the shelf and putting them back in the wrong place, soiling pages and that sort of thing. And we do catch some even tearing pages from the books, trying to sneak books out of the library without permission. You name it; I've seen it all."

"Yeah, yeah, I get it. That's certainly not me," Kyle said in a huff as he walked off.

The three walked out into the hall, turned left, and there were the elevators, just as the Eye had said, but more of them than Kyle had ever seen.

"Oh, damn it, he didn't tell me which one," he said, turning to the others.

"Maybe it doesn't matter," they replied.

"It's like I'm stuck in my life's vocation and living my life all over again. Don't get me wrong, I love libraries, but not 24/7. God, I sure as hell hope I wake up one of these days."

"Don't get ahead of yourself," WORD said.

They got on one of the elevators, and Kyle keyed in the number he thought the Eye had given him earlier. The elevator doors closed and the elevator moved very smoothly, and Kyle thought how pleasant the ride was. It seemed to him the doors opened to an aisle filled with books, and he thought he could hear, "You have arrived at your selected destination," announced by the elevator. Kyle then glided into the aisle and he was amazed to see that the spine of each book was really a door. He didn't realize that he was alone and floating! There, right in front of him, the very first book was *The Tales of Canterbury* by Geoffery Chaucer! He was aghast and as he was taking this in, he noticed over the door were the words, Middle English.

"I blew it," he said, turning around and looking for WORD and THOUGHT, but they were nowhere in sight. "I'm in the wrong section," he muttered to himself, "Where are those two? I must have done something wrong in the elevator. But, oh, *The Tales of Canterbury*, I must take a peek," and just as he put his hand on the doorknob, the Eye appeared right above him.

"Where do you think you're going?" the Eye asked.

"I just want to take a look. Isn't that okay?"

"Oh, yes, it's okay, but you have to be careful, it's really easy to get lost here. I'm sure you've heard of getting 'lost in a book'! No doubt you've heard or even read the story of *Robinson Crusoe*. He's one who got lost in a book," the Eye warned.

"What are you talking about? That was fiction, a story by Daniel Defoe," Kyle protested.

"Yes, but few people realize it's based on a real person and it was Defoe who rescued him with his imagination and immortalized him in the book. There was a lot of confusion about just who was the real Robinson Crusoe, after the book came out. So, as I say, be careful or you may never get to find Remedial Grammar."

"Don't worry. I don't want to be stuck in this place!" Kyle grumbled.

As Kyle went through the door, he found himself in front of an old Elizabethan building and there, directly in front of him, was the sign, *Tabard Inn*. Of course, he couldn't resist, so thereupon he opened the tavern door and there, in front of him, was a company of men and women, the likes of which he had never seen. He immediately went to a table where a little man, who looked quite comfortable, was sitting, sipping from a metal mug while copying from some notes and writing in a tablet. As he took his seat he said hello to the man, but was totally ignored as the man kept on writing. Kyle looked over onto the tablet where the man was writing, but he was having great difficulty reading, it all seemed so strange. At the top was written:

Here bygynneth the
book of the
tales of Caunterbury

Whan that Aprill with his shoures soote

The droghte of March hath perced to the roote,
And bathed every veyne in swich licour
Of which vertu engendred is the flour…

At first he couldn't believe what he was reading, as he was confused and when he spoke to the stranger he acted as though Kyle wasn't even there.

All of a sudden Kyle was overcome with a sense of awe. "Of course," he thought, "it's Middle English, and that's Chaucer himself, who was one of the first major writers to publish his work in Middle English."

Just then the man looked up and said, "Hello, are you talking to me?"

"Yes, I was. I'm Kyle Wilson, and I was just saying, hello. I'm wondering what you're writing?"

"Well, I'm Geoffrey, Geoffrey Chaucer, that is. In answer to your question I'm transcribing these tales of a pilgrimage from London to Canterbury that took place with a group of pilgrims in April."

"Oh, yes, I read about them when I was a student," Kyle replied.

"Well, what did you think?"

"I really couldn't make much of them," Kyle replied. "They seemed like such a disreputable and ugly bunch of people!"

"That's mostly true, but I thought that was the idea. You know, showing them for who and what they really are! Except for the old Knight, they really were a deplorable folk. Now the Parson, that's a whole other story in itself, but I choose not go there."

"What's so different about the Parson?" Kyle asked.

"Careful what you ask for! Attack the church, are you crazy? I'm just trying to promote the vernacular. I don't want to be pilloried or burnt at the stake. No, we won't go there!"

"How is it anyway that you talk in regular English, but you're writing in Middle English?" Kyle asked.

"What do you think? I've always been ahead of my time, but that motley crew doesn't understand anything else and that's the way they speak too!" Chaucer said. "I just tell it like it is or was, as the case may be, except for the Parson, of course. Oh, I suppose I could write in French as most others do, but then I'm not just anyone else, am I?"

"I have to say," he went on, "it's quite a trek from here to Canterbury. If you're headed that way, I can give you some helpful tips."

"No thanks. I have to run," Kyle said, then thinking to himself, "Talk about getting lost in a book! I'm getting out of here, this is too creepy for me." He said goodbye, got up, glided back out of the tavern, through the door, and back into the library.

Back inside, he started floating along the aisle. After going along for what seemed forever in one direction, he spied the book *Beowulf,* the epic poem that had always intrigued him, but by then he also realized that he was lost again. He was getting anxious, and those other voices…

"He seems to be restless doctor—his pressure is slightly elevated and his pulse is racing," a voice said.

"Just keep an eye on him."

"Yes, Doctor."

The voices faded and Kyle was thinking about his dilemma. What was it going to take to get back to his regular world or was he going to be stuck in Limbo forever?

"Hey, Kyle, wake up, we're here," THOUGHT and WORD called to him as the elevator doors opened.

"But where are we and where have you two been?" Kyle cried. "I thought we had already arrived, and you two just disappeared."

"No, no, you just fell asleep," WORD said.

"Asleep?" Kyle wondered.

"Yes," WORD said.

"That was so weird, such a strange dream. I felt like I was sleepwalking or something. I can't quite put my finger on it, how mysterious." Kyle mused.

"Haven't you ever dreamt that you're dreaming?" WORD asked.

As they stepped into the aisle, they could see the sign, *Virtual Section.*

"What's this?" Kyle asked. "I thought we were going to the section on Modern English."

"What did you expect?" THOUGHT replied. "You used the computer and unless you specified that you wanted books your request automatically defaulted to the virtual library. Of course, if you want to, you can always go back upstairs and use the card catalog or, if you use the computer, you should specifically ask for bound books."

"No, no! Let's get on with it," Kyle insisted in a disgusted tone. All he could think of was his overriding dilemma. How was he going get on and where would he find a way back to his own world?"

Looking along down the aisle, all Kyle could see were booths, something like study carrels, only they were somewhat bigger and each had what appeared to be a computer, but with a helmet and two hand-holds in addition to a mouse and keyboard.

"So what's the deal here?" Kyle asked.

"Well, you can pick any one of the booths, look up the subject or item you want and then put the helmet on and grab the hand-holds. Using the buttons, you will automatically be immersed in that specific area. You control your movement within the book or video with the finger controls, and you can stop any time by just removing your hands, which will free you to leave or to look up another item," WORD said, and then he continued, "THOUGHT and I are going to leave you for a bit as we have other business to attend to. We'll catch up with you later."

As Kyle settled into an empty booth nearby, his two companions sauntered off down the aisle.

THE UNDERWORLD

After his friends left, Kyle started his search for Modern English Grammar, but since he didn't really think he needed remedial study, he was only halfheartedly searching for grammar. He began nosing around to satisfy his curiosity.

Soon he noticed a title that piqued his curiosity, *Shades of Virgil's Aeneid*. Remembering Aeneas' quest to find his father, Kyle decided to take a look, thinking of his own father's two extended episodes in a coma.

Putting on the helmet, he grabbed the handholds and pressed the start button. Immediately, he was immersed in a virtual world and found himself on the banks of a river, and standing there, he was reminded of Aeneas' journey to the underworld to find his father to learn of his own purpose and future.

"Surely an act of desperation, but what have I got to lose, and how ironic," Kyle thought, as he looked out across the river. Then thinking of his own father, what had he endured when he was in his comas? He wondered how his father had managed to rejoin his family and the world of the living after his two long periods of oblivion?

Standing there on the riverbank with the mist rising off the river, he could hear the rippling of water and shortly through the mist he could vaguely see a boat wending its way towards him. As the boat came slowly into view, Kyle could see the figure of the same man he had seen depicted in a scene of *The Last Judgement*, by Michelangelo in the Sistine chapel; could it really be Charon? It had been awe inspiring when he saw the original painting, but now, "how demonic looking," he thought, as the boat pulled up and beached on the sand.

"Get in," he said.

"Are you really Charon? I don't have a golden bough to ransom my way," Kyle said.

As they pushed off, with the abrasive sound of the sand and the rippling of water, the *ferryman* said, "Yeah, I'm Charon, and, in case you don't know, I don't stand on ceremony. Don't believe all the rumors you hear about having to pay to cross the Styx. Why would I lay up material treasure when I'm caught here between two worlds, where worldly goods have no value? But I do hope you know this is a one-way journey."

"What? You mean I can't come back. Others like Aeneas, Odysseus and Orpheus did; why can't I?"

"Sorry, but you're not one of the heroes from the ancient world. You'll have to make the best of it in the underworld. Although it is rumored that others have gone back to the world of the living from that side of the Stix, but it's nothing that I have anything to do with," he said, as he beached on the other shore.

A sense of loneliness and foreboding came over Kyle as they landed. On the shore a haze hung over the land, stretching off to the horizon. As he exited the boat, through the haze he could see a faint figure who looked like a person, but transparent, who said, "I'm from the souls of the departed and here to guide you? Who are you looking for and where are you going?"

Remembering the difference between Tartarus, the place of punishment, and Elysium, the place for those chosen to live a blessed and happy life after death, Kyle said, "I'm looking for my father in Elysium."

The soul told him the path that he must take if he was to be successful.

Directions in mind, Kyle set off and like Aeneas, found himself among the wailing souls of dead infants, then to the spirits of the erroneously executed and onto the suicides, where he was confronted by a soul who looked hauntingly familiar and frightening, as he tried to hurry past.

"Will you not stop for a moment?" the soul asked.

"Should I know you? I'm in a hurry to find my father."

"Could it be that you don't recognize me?"

Kyle stopped in his tracks and directly looked at his inquisitor, "Oh my God, how can you be here?" he asked, as he realized this was a shade of himself out of his troubled past, though quite a bit younger looking.

"Yeah, I'm not surprised that you'd want to avoid me. Except for that awful gash on your head, you seem to be in a much better humor since you sent me here years ago," the shade said.

Automatically reaching to his head and feeling the wound, "I'm sorry," Kyle said, "I was totally without control and so despondent back then. But I had no idea that I had created something like this. Why are you here, since I never successfully completed the deed, as it were?"

"I hope you can admit that you died a little each time you tried to leave the world of the living. In your naïveté your soul took a beating. I'm here as a testament to your past self-destruction, something that I surely hope remains in the past. I know you now look forward to unraveling your own purpose and future."

"Yes, years of therapy left me with an appreciation of life, now only to find that I'm trapped in a state where I'm really not living, but I'm not dead either. Somehow I transitioned to a Land of Letters and Words. It's like I'm in Limbo or something. Of course, everything was black and white back then; there were no half measures or remedies, so when I became despondent, I saw only one solution – suicide. Now I have to look back on those episodes and put them with many other actions that I'm ashamed of," Kyle said.

"I suppose it was a reasonable action because you didn't know any better then and didn't know how to cope, but it doesn't excuse you either. Now that you've learned how to get on in the world, you must accept and own that behavior as a part of you and move on to find your purpose in the world," the shade said and then disappeared.

Kyle continued, following the same path and passing through the other realms until he stood before gates, clearly inscribed, ELYSIUM. Beyond was an area of beautiful meadows, just as told in the *Aeneid*, and extending as far as he could see. Standing at the gates were two souls, as though they were waiting for new additions.

"I'm looking for my father. Can you help me find him?" Kyle asked.

"You've come to the right place. Come on in."

As Kyle walked in, he immediately felt different. He looked down at himself and gasped. He was as transparent as the souls standing there.

"What happened; what's going on?" he cried.

"You're now officially dead," a soul said.

"What? I never expected this. What am I going to do? This is worse than a coma," Kyle bemoaned.

"In case you never heard, it's called the law of unintended consequences. But patience. Surely you didn't think you'd come to the underworld in regular form, did you?"

Kyle turned to go back through the gates, but they had disappeared.

Throwing up his arms in futility he exclaimed, "Well, hell, I'm here now. I might as well get on with it. Where do I find my father?"

"Just follow the path and look for the soul searcher."

Frustrated, Kyle struck out and, in not more than several hundred feet, signposts appeared at a fork in the path. One read, HEROES. The other, UNSUNG HEROES.

In spite of his frustration, he mused, "The path to UNSUNG HEROES, that's a no brainer," and he set off again. As he rounded a large group of trees, he came out overlooking a beautiful valley, and everywhere he looked there were groups of souls either sitting in little areas or standing in groups. Walking up to one of the souls, Kyle said, "I'm looking for the soul searcher to help me find my father."

He was directed to another soul, who looked like a priest even though he still appeared transparent, like the other souls.

Walking up to the priest, Kyle said, "I hear you're the one I need to see to help me find someone."

"What do you think this is? Don't you know this is the eternal resting place of the Unsung Heroes?" the Priest admonished.

"I'm sorry, but I'm looking for my father. I need to see him to apologize and he may have some vital information for me."

"What do you think an apology is worth here? If he's here for peace and quiet, like the rest of us, he won't care one little bit for such drivel. I mean what's the use of it to him? He's already gotten his resting place assured and an apology will get him nothing."

"Well, of course, but I guess it would make me feel better," Kyle said. "I also have some very important questions to ask him."

"This ought to be good. Let's hear it then."

"I need to ask him how he regained consciousness from comas he endured, not to mention, of course, I do so want to see him to tell him I'm sorry for how I treated him in his last years."

"What did you do? Were you unkind?"

"Yes, I had tried for so long to help him in one form or another, but I now realize I was really trying to dictate the course of his life and, of course, I failed miserably. In fact, it could be my browbeating that may have driven him to his second seizure and coma. Maybe he'll forgive me, but even worse, I think, is when I had to put him in a nursing home and I pretty much abandoned him there."

"Seems like you're putting a lot on yourself."

"I know, even the Doctor said that dad's seizures and resulting comas were idiopathic in nature, but I still can't help myself," Kyle said.

"Are you sure you just aren't giving in to your own guilt?"

"Maybe for being overbearing, but I can't excuse the way I pretty much abandoned him after he went to the nursing home."

"Objectively, I'd say you did pretty well by him. You did, after all, help to take care of his personal needs, didn't you?" the priest asked.

"I know, but it was so hard to visit him there. He hated it so much and, when I did go, he'd bemoan his lot and he'd beg me not to leave. It just tore me up inside. Needless to say, I didn't visit much!"

"Sounds pretty human to me. Don't beat yourself up so much. So, what made you think he'd be with the unsung-heroes, anyway?"

"If any man was ever a hero, it was my dad. He suffered hell on earth and yet he carried on. He certainly ranks as one of the unsung heroes. In spite of his personal demons, and he had plenty of them, he got up every day, did his job and provided for his family. He did all this separated from his family and living alone for the most part, only seeing his family on weekends. Anyway, let's get on. We're here so let's go find him."

"Are you sure you want to do this? Just how long do you think they would call it paradise, if every Tom, Dick and Harry dropped by to pester their ancestors. No, the Elysian Fields are there for those who rightly earned eternal rest and peace, without the likes of you disturbing them on every whim."

"Look, as I've already said, aside from apologizing, I have to ask him how he recovered from the two different comas he endured."

"Didn't you ever think of a living apology?"

"What do you mean?"

"You don't really believe saying you're sorry is worth your breath, do you? Don't you think, that instead of some maudlin, groveling for forgiveness and trying to appease your own sense of guilt, that changing your behavior would be more what your father would want for you? In other words, get on with your life, be more honest with yourself and act consistently with what you say and promote, and have the guts to live with the consequences of your actions?"

"That's easy for you to say, but the experience with my dad, putting him in the nursing home, that's not something I can easily put aside. Looking back on it, I should have made myself visit and just endured his pleadings. Now I guess I'm just left with my feelings; hindsight is 20/20 and there's not much else I can do about it."

"That's right, there's nothing you can do to change the past, but instead of wishing for a different outcome, you can really assert yourself to change your behavior, and it's a great start to just acknowledge your part in the things that trouble you. At the same time be objective about the circumstances that transpired, not least about the things that impinged on you during that time," the priest said.

"More to that other point about gleaning from your father how he revived from his comas, why do you think he'll even have the right answer for you, anyway? Isn't it enough to know he did it, and don't you think you should find your own way? I think it's a much better idea to find your own solution to the riddles in your life, instead of tilting at windmills or visiting the dead and other unfounded solutions that appeal to a sense of false hope, deluding you to think you're actually coping when you're not."

"So you're telling me there's no point in seeing my father? What the hell! After coming all this way, I can't just leave without seeing him," Kyle said.

"Not so fast. Like most from your world, many if not most of their problems are of their own making, and getting out of them is frequently not so easy," the Priest said.

"I still want to see my dad!" Kyle announced. "I'll exit afterwards. Besides if you're so smart where do I start and how do I find the souls of Unsung Heroes?"

"Alright, alright, you start right here and maybe you'll learn something useful, but I hope you realize this is going to be a onetime visit," the Priest said. "I also hope you know that you need to be out of here by midnight tomorrow!"

"Or else?" Kyle asked

"You'll find you're a permanent resident on this side of the river, that's what. Of course, I can't say where you'll end up, but I can pretty much guarantee it won't be with the Unsung Heroes."

"Oh my God, then let's get on with it before I'm stuck," Kyle was getting anxious.

"Who are you and where are you from?" the priest asked in a resigned tone.

"Kyle Wilson, from Hanover, New Hampshire."

"Father's name?"

"Sidney Wilson from Manchester, Vermont."

The Priest then performed an incantation, "I command you now to rise, Sidney Wilson, to meet your past, in the here and now!"

Then and there a soul appeared from out of the ether.

"Why have I been summoned?" the soul asked.

"Someone is here to see you," the priest said, pointing to Kyle.

"A visitor, you've got to be kidding," Sydney replied.

"It's me, father," Kyle, said, "I'm so sorry for the way I treated you at the end. I just couldn't bear those visits. They really got to me. I want you to know I still loved you back then, I just couldn't bear what had become of you."

"Come, son," stretching out his arms to embrace Kyle, "that was then and this is now. What of a world of circuitous paths that each of us must traverse on our journey to eternity? I've come to learn that each one has his own journey, no two are alike."

"But, dad can you forgive me for how I treated you after you retired and especially when you were in the nursing home?"

"Son, if it means that much to you, of course, I forgive you, but is that really worth anything to you? You see I can easily forgive, because that is of no consequence to me now. It's you who have to forgive yourself, become a better man, someone that you can respect and fully accept with an imperfect past. After all, the journey of life is exactly that, what we become is the past of our former selves that we struggle to put right, sometimes referred to as personal growth."

"For me, son, every day I thank my lucky stars that I'm not over there with the Heroes. You see, they may have done the things that others believed were great, that they shaped the world in some profound or significant way. But when they arrive at the Fields of Heroes, many of them find they were shallow egotists, so here they must suffer for the things they did not do, because that's the price we all pay. It's either the bad things that we did to others that we never put behind us, or the things we wanted to do, but never did. Maybe we were afraid or lazy; these are the regrets and are best summed up by the great poet, John Greenleaf Whittier, who said, *For all sad words of tongue and pen, the saddest are these, it might have been.* I can tell you right now most of the heroes I've known have a lot to answer for."

"Thanks, Dad, that's a lot to hash over, but the other thing I want to ask is when you had your seizures and went into comas, how did you manage to come out of them? Was it something you consciously did, something you had a part in that allowed you to regain consciousness?"

"Son, now why do you want to know something stupid like that?"

"It's not stupid, Dad. In fact, I'm in a coma right now and I need to know how I can help myself, and I just thought you might be able to give me a tip or two."

"All I can tell you, son, is what happened to me. Let me tell you it wasn't very easy either, and it's nothing like what you've been going through. I can see now how you've been wrapped up with letters and words. God, I should have never let your mother's family take you kids, but what the hell was I supposed to do, with your mother having to be put away? Anyway, with that pseudo, intellectual family of hers, it must have been hell on you; they sure were great talkers, with lots of words and fancy language—three women at that, with the only man in the house, an old man, your grandfather. I'm sure they laid a few trips on you that have been hell to live with. Of course, all that religiosity of your mother, especially after she got sick. That couldn't have been easy on you either."

"Jesus, Dad, how did you deal with it?"

"Son, plain and simple, I loved her to my very core! No one is perfect and she had so many wonderful qualities. Not to mention we were both on the same wavelength on so many things. You know when you boil it down, it seemed to me that she knew for sure what all the rest wrestle with in continuous doubt."

"But, to your question, the coma was different for me, being a farm boy, growing up dirt poor, and then, of course my mother..." Tears came to his eyes. "I still can't bear to think of it."

"Anyway, you know I always had a thing with animals, being a herdsman, not to mention a college degree in Animal Husbandry. Anyway, in my comas I found myself in a land of animals, with many, if not all of them, running the show. Probably the biggest thing I learned was I was not in charge. I'm sure you've noticed that animals just do their thing. They don't fret about tomorrow. Sure, birds build their nests and lions make their dens, but they trust in an outcome that's somehow written into their genes and they don't worry about the unforeseen. Occasionally, an unhappy fate does catch them unawares and sometimes even extinguishes some of them, but in the interim they get on with their lives, living to their fullest potential."

"In other words, try as I might, being in that other kingdom, I lived according to their dictates. On the one hand, I tried to be myself and express my reason for being, but I also learned acceptance. So, in answer to your question, Kyle, I left when it was time. One day I just felt relaxed and particularly self-possessed, and poof, I woke up!"

"Jesus, Dad, thanks, but that's not much help. I guess as usual I'm left on my own."

"One more question, Dad."

"Get on with it then, son. I'm not disposed to being interrupted these days."

"Is this all there is, Dad? What do you do all day?"

"I do whatever I damn well please, that's what I do, but why do you ask? After all, this is your coma and your own mess to figure out – we all get our own messes, you know. Now, you take care of yourself and have a good life," he said and then just vanished.

"So much for that," Kyle mumbled and turned to the priest who was standing nearby. "You certainly had my dad's take on things, so guess I better get on. Can you tell me how I get out of here?"

"Isn't it just like you mortals, you get yourself in a pickle and then you expect someone else to get you out. All I can tell you is continue on the path that led you here and keep an eye out for the jumping off place and remember you've got 24… well 20 hours left now."

Kyle rushed to get back on the path, but he was feeling subdued. "Jesus, what a letdown," he thought.

Other voices intruded and then that megaphone sound, "Calling Dr. Norris, report to ICU—Room three."

"What is it, Dick?" Kyle heard.

"Hi Brad, looks like Kyle here is not doing so well. It's been two weeks and nothing from him. Just wondering if you concur on moving him to Pine View Nursing Home for custodial care? I was surprised at your chart notes, regarding his coma-scale responses," Dr. Angle said.

"Yeah he's comatose all right. Only scored a seven when I did an evaluation yesterday. Any lower and he'd be brain-dead! If he comes around, it's up to him at this point and it'll have to be one of those rare spontaneous responses."

"Jesus, Brad, PVS (persistent vegetative state), that bad, huh?"

"No, Dick. It's a little early to say that, but he could be heading there. I'm sorry to say, but his *no eye-opening response* to speech or pain was a 1; his *verbal response* – with only incomprehensible sounds, to prodding, was a 2; and his *motor response* –withdrawal from pain was only a 4. He's a solid 7 and I don't think we can do any more for him."

"I hate shipping him out so early, but we need the bed. Of course, we can always bring him back if he rallies," Dr. Angle said.

"Of course, and he may yet come around, but we usually give 'em a full three months before declaring PVS," Dr. Norris said.

"Jesus, they're throwing me under the bus already," Kyle screamed in his mind, accidently letting go of the handholds of the VR console.

"Hey Brad, did you see his hands just twitch?" Dr. Angle said.

"Totally involuntary, Dick. I'd say just send him and I'll call the family to let them know."

"I'll have Bernese call for transport ASAP," Dr. Angle said.

TOWER OF BABEL

Kyle grabbed the handholds again, but to his surprise he was back at the opening screen of the console. He laughed.

"I'd bet that's the easiest anyone ever came back from the underworld. At least I'm back where I began, but Jesus, what a mess. I guess I'll just go along like dad did and hope for the best. The bastards that run this hospital sure as hell aren't any help. What's next, the undertaker?"

He began nosing around again and very shortly he noticed a title that piqued his curiosity, *Words in Modern Interpretations of the Biblical Literature*.

Suddenly something violently shook him.

"Bernese, can you get the other corner of the drawsheet," a man's voice said.

"God he's heavy."

"Yeah, this is my second vegetable this morning," the man said.

"Please, Henry, don't talk like that. Sometimes they can hear you," she scolded as they settled Kyle on the gurney.

"Feels like I'm flying. Oops, now I've done it," Kyle simultaneously thought, while being moved and accidently pressing the start button on the hand-holds of the VR.

"Hey, it's a persistent vegetative state, no matter how you slice it and they're always heavy, so sign the release and I'll be off," the transport man said.

"A God-damn, vegetable, really. I wish that rude bastard could be in my place for five minutes! Besides, who the hell's this guy to make a diagnosis like that?"

Then movement followed by more noise, as Kyle could feel his gurney moving in different directions and sounds of different doors. Momentary stillness, followed by a car engine starting and then movement again, but in quiet...

Kyle's attention suddenly shifted as he found himself in an eerie undefined hallway, but with an open door directly in front and a figure standing just inside that looked like the souls he had just met in the underworld. As he walked in, he was overwhelmed as the soul rushed over to him and threw her transparent arms around him. "Kyle! My boy. I'm so glad to see you, but why have you come?"

He was totally taken aback! "Mother, is it really you?" he cried.

"It is only my essence that remains, but, yes the Lord works in mysterious ways."

"Oh God!" Immediately, Kyle's conflicting emotions of long past feelings about his mother sprang up within him.

"How is it you're here, Mother?"

"The real question is why are you here, my Boy? It's long before your time, my Child. Tell me what is wrong."

He became totally confused, mumbling, "Oh, Mother, I have no idea. I've been trapped in places with letters, words, and in strange worlds. Now finding you here in this strange land, I have lost any sense of where and who I really am."

His mind recoiled and the conflict with his mother that had haunted him all his life, rose out of the memories of his childhood and teenage years and overwhelmed him. He thought of many occasions, of disputes, situations and conversations with her. They often had ended up with her profound personal solution, so frequently announced as "God will decide," or with a paraphrase from the Bible. There was no argument that could penetrate her thinking. Any objective response would only be confronted with her infallible, subjective truth of the scripture!

Now as an adult he fully understood why this had been such a conflict for him. It was his deep and abiding love for this beautiful creature who had nourished him, read endlessly to him and fostered in him her belief that he could do no wrong in her eyes. Her unconditional love for him had been absolute. No matter how he might confront what he perceived as her illogical notions, she replied with gentleness, and with absolute faith in her beliefs.

"Son, it can be no accident that you're here in the midst of the Biblical literature. In and through my faith, I know that all of us must confront the demons that haunt us in life, in one form or another. So it is that your conflicts have brought you to my domain where I sit on the right-hand of God. As the great prophet Luke said, … *joy shall be in heaven over one sinner that repenteth, more than over ninety and nine just persons, which need no repentance.*"[3]

"But, Mother, I don't know what I've done. Suddenly, I just overheard, while in some hospital bed, *of some kind of*

---

[3]   Luke, 15:7, King James Version of the Holy Bible (KJV)

accident, and poof I am abruptly in Limbo, what some jerk called a persistent vegetative state."

"I wonder what your father would have to say about this. He had two long periods of coma and seemed to survive, after a fashion that is. Pity you can't ask him; he might have some good advice."

"Mysteriously, I did get to talk with him and all he could say was that he awoke when he fully regained his composure and became self-possessed. I can't imagine how that can be helpful."

"Son, as Paul the apostle says, *you won't be given more than you can handle and God won't allow you to be tested with more than you can deal with, but that he will provide an escape.*"[4]

"Mother, why do you insist on these religious solutions to everything? Why couldn't you just love me and treat me like all my friends were treated? All that stuff made me feel so different from the other boys. I hate to say it, but as much as I loved you, I was ashamed to bring any friends home because of how odd and different our home seemed to me."

"Son, as much as I loved you, more than life itself, I could put no thing before God; for you, yourself, are but a gift from God!"

"Mother, please. Childhood was so wonderful otherwise, like one continued fantasy with your reading and your presence, putting us all, including the adults, on a special plane where you occupied a special place."

"Son, I hope you realize my sisters treated me like a child when I came back home. As a grown woman and mother, they relegated me to a child's role, and their love and acceptance of me in that place became my burden for survival, even as they became mothers to my children, but, of course, only in a

---

4   Paul, I Corinthians, 10:13, KJV

matriarchal or custodial sense. It was I who brought to you all the spirit of the soul and the ways of the world. Nature in her rustic beauty was my schoolroom and the knowledge of the larger world was our subject; God provided."

Background sounds suddenly intruded, "Katrina, this is Henry, Transport four, arriving at Pine Valley."

"Go ahead, four."

"I'll be dropping patient Kyle Wilson and returning to base."

"Okay, Henry. It's busy here; you may get another call before you get here."

Kyle's sense of motion suddenly stopped. Inadvertently, he momentarily let go the hand-holds. He heard a slamming of metal doors, then a sense of flying again and more banging of doors.

"We'll take him from here," a husky woman's voice said. He felt himself strangely moving yet again and then the husky woman's voice. Joyce, tell Bill and Walt to come to room A-5 for a transfer."

"Yes, ma'am."

Kyle felt himself suddenly changing direction and more voices, "Walt, ready on three; one, two, three."

Kyle briefly sensed a flying motion and then a momentary stillness as he sunk into something soft.

"God, they don't get any lighter, do they?"

"Goes with the territory."

"Kyle, can you hear me?" a woman's silken, voice asked. "Nothing, huh dear? We'll get Doctor Swanson down here to check you out…"

Footsteps receded, then stillness…

The VR screen, with *Words in Modern Interpretations of the Biblical Literature,* was in front of him again.

"I suppose Mother will be here somewhere," he thought, as he grabbed the hand-holds again.

But he was confronted with a door directly in front of him with an inscription over the top, *Table of Contents.* As he walked into the room, he could see there were just more doors with inscriptions over them, each door representing a different chapter of the Bible.

"God, my earlier dream with the Eye telling me about getting lost in a book now seems so long ago, but that was really prescient. I'll never find my way back to the front of this book!" Then Kyle chuckled as he thought, "Of course, I can always just let go..."

The very first door on Kyle's left had the inscription *Genesis*, so he decided to try it and once inside he was amazed to see the different sub-sections of *Genesis*. Once again he was confronted with yet another series of doors where he noticed a door with the inscription *Tower of Babel.*

"I've always wondered about that story," he thought to himself as he stepped through the doorway into the room. There in front of him was a huge conference table with all these strange objects sitting around it, talking with one another.

"Obviously more words," Kyle thought.

"Come in, come in and take a seat," said the one that looked like a burning bush and seated at the head of the table.

As Kyle sat down he noticed in front of each seat was a place card, and then he noticed the card in front of him read VISITING RELIGION. He looked around at the other place cards. RELIGION, EPISTEMOLOGY, PHENOMENOLOGY, FAITH, LANGUAGE, HERESY, PAROCHIALITY and ENLIGHTENMENT filled all the other chairs around the table, with the word GOD sitting at the head of the table.

"Please tell us what brings you here and what religion that you represent," GOD said, looking directly at Kyle.

Kyle was totally flummoxed, "In the first place I'm looking for a way out from the places and worlds I've recently been finding myself trapped in. Secondly, I came here because it's an area of Biblical study that I've always been curious about, and I just sat here when you asked me to take a seat."

"Well then, you're supposed to be here. You should know by now that nothing happens here by accident. So tell us what religion you practice," GOD said.

"I'm a Protestant, and brought up a Congregationalist, but not necessarily a practicing one, you know. Oh, I do go to church sometimes for social occasions, like to hear Christmas carols or at Easter."

"Why such a lackluster attendance? How is it you're a non-believer?" GOD asked. "We know it was not for want of a proper upbringing. I know your mother was a tireless promoter of the *word*. But we do seem to be getting more non-believers lately."

"Well, I guess you could say I'm a bit of an agnostic. None of that religious stuff makes any real sense to me. Pardon my effrontery, but who speaks for our Lord anyway? All my childhood I heard about the angels and the saints, but I could never see that any of that talk helped me, at least, not in any personal sense. I don't mean to be rude, but why should we believe Jehovah spoke to Moses, giving him the Ten Commandments, or for that matter that he ever speaks to anyone? Oh, I know many say that the Lord speaks to them, as my own mother and others in the past have said that he spoke to them."

"Are you calling Moses a liar? You better watch your mouth! Around here we're careful not to insult anyone's belief," RELIGION said.

"No, I'm not intending to insult anyone at all. I think Moses thought Jehovah did speak to him and my mother did as well, for that matter! But I can't see that it ever did her any good. She became an oddity and marked as unstable, in her own family. I'll give her one thing, she stuck to her beliefs no matter. I just have a hard time believing that Jehovah, if he even exits, ever actually speaks to anyone. By now it's a known fact that ancient peoples didn't know thoughts originated in their own heads, so any complicated thoughts were attributed to the supernatural," Kyle said.

"Well, Son, don't you find it the least bit interesting that belief in Jehovah not only sustained your mother, but infused her with the rapture of the divine presence?" GOD asked.

"What's going on here anyway? I thought this section was supposed to be about the Tower of Babel? That is what I was really interested in checking out," Kyle said.

"Look Sonny, don't get cute with us! Just exactly what are you trying to say? We all know the story. It's summarized right up there on the wall," RELIGION said, pointing with his head to a place on the wall, across the table in front of him.

Kyle looked up to the spot and there in bold letters was the *Tower* story, *telling how originally, the whole world had one language; people in their prideful actions were usurping the place of Lord by building a tower to heaven. The Lord saw that with this act nothing was beyond them, so he deliberately confused their language and scattered them across the earth...*[5]

Interrupting Kyle's reading, GOD asked, "What is it about the Tower that interests you, not to mention the quarrel with your mother, of course? I do think they're linked at a very primal level."

"Well, I've always wondered why the world is such a confusing place, and this seemed like one of the places that was maybe at the heart of it all. You know all the different nationalities, customs, languages and just plain English words themselves, as well," Kyle said. "It seems awfully contrary to me that the Lord would purposefully make his creation more confusing than it was originally, and for what purpose?"

---

[5]   Genesis, Tower of Babel, Verses, 11-9, KJV.

"You really are a 'doubting Thomas.' Apparently, this really does have its roots in your childhood," GOD remarked.

FAITH then interrupted saying, "You should know by now, ours is not to question the Lord's handiwork. Didn't they teach you this in Sunday School? Now it appears you obviously lack faith and trust that the Lord of all creation knows what he's doing. How is it anyway, with your puny ego and intellect, that you expect to understand these things, their origins and their purpose for being?" FAITH asked.

"That's just it, I don't understand, but I haven't seen any reasonable explanation either. Just because some printed book or some preacher or a gazillion other people say it's so, doesn't make it so, especially if it doesn't make any sense. Besides, with all the different gods for all the different religions, why would one supreme God allow all those other opposing views and beliefs to exist, with each religion professing theirs as the true path of salvation, in one form or another? How on earth, if one was really searching for the one right religion, would one know which one to choose? So often I think of my mother and the problems this caused for her, making her an oddity in her own family." Kyle said.

At this PHENOMENOLOGY said, "As a representative of the subjective world, I find our visitor's reflections very stimulating, and I would only add that if the Lord gives one free will and if man, with his many languages, is representative of the Lord's handiwork, why then would anyone choose a 'false God'? Our visitor's experience in this world has not shown him any good reason to believe that the experiences of others, regarding the intangible essence of creation, are any better than his own. If he himself were to experience a miracle or if Jehovah were to speak directly to him, then he might change his mind, but until that time occurs, I believe he is totally justified in his position."

At this GOD addressed the group. "I know you all give special weight to the things I say. So, let me state categorically that I do not know of any one or other different spokesmen who speak for the Lord or Jehovah. Many profess to speak, claiming firsthand knowledge of a specific God or an aspect of his manifestations. But if it were the Lord's wish, with all the power that's been attributed to him, he could easily make himself visible or accessible to all. **I must remind you all that as the word GOD, I am not the Lord God, and the things attributed to me are not necessarily the Lord speaking directly through me in any given language! In other words, I take no authorship of what's so often attributed to me.** However, I say to you, Kyle, might it not be that like so many who have come before you, that God may just be testing you as he did with the likes of Job, Jonah and certainly, not least, your mother and that in his time, if he deems you worthy, he will reveal himself to you as well?"

After GOD'S assertions, EPISTEMOLOGY jumped into the discussion.

"While doubt was always a factor, it is particularly evident in light of the gradual erosion of the anchors and attitudes that once were the backbone or justifications for all the myths that have existed throughout history. From the time of the Inquisition when Galileo showed that the earth was not the center of the universe; from Newton who showed that reason and science could explain physical phenomena, formerly attributed to the supernatural; from Darwin who explained evolution, giving rise to understanding mankind's real origins; from Freud who uncovered the unconscious, again dispelling the supernatural; and, of course, in our own time Einstein who changed the concepts of space, time and gravity--all have brought new knowledge that demythologizes the age-old myths, putting the underpinnings of all the world's religions in peril. To this day it is true that many, many individuals cling to their religious beliefs, dismissing all evidence to the contrary, and they continue to believe there is an essence of their particular religion that contains the ultimate truth and their subsequent salvation."

With a loud cry, HERESY yelled, "Stop! This is blasphemy. Have you no shame? In our own time, because of the very things you have enumerated, man's search for meaning and purpose are even more profoundly needed than any other time in history. If man is alienated from himself and his fellow man, then isn't it obvious the missing ingredient is faith? We all know the scripture is sacred. It is not up for questioning or debate; it is *the word* as the Lord has presented it to us. We must live according to its tenets if we want eternal salvation! These new truths that EPISTEMOLOGY enumerated should really serve only to bolster our faith, since they merely explain man's gifts and the intricacy of our beautiful world that the Lord has given us! They should help bolster our purpose and belief in Jehovah."

"I say Amen to that, Kyle, your mother was certainly one of the Lord's devout supporters," FAITH exclaimed.

"And you, GOD, how can you go on in such a manner?" HERESY exclaimed.

"What can I say," GOD said, "I am who I am!"

"So now you're mocking the Lord?" FAITH asked.

"I'm not mocking anyone. I'm just being myself," GOD said.

"Yeah, just being your natural sarcastic self," HERESY said.

At this LANGUAGE piped up, "HERESY, aren't you and FAITH being a bit parochial. So, GOD is using the same words as Jehovah did when describing himself to Moses. Big deal! And Jehovah himself, how was he to describe himself, with a grunt or some other unintelligible gesture? No, of course not, he supposedly used language, the very thing he then set out to confuse by supposedly creating many tongues. I think it's you religious folks who have confused things."

Kyle piped up, "This is the very conundrum I'm talking about. If Jehovah is within us, then doesn't it seem only logical that we should each be that thing—*ourselves*—that he has created?"

"Son, are your current trials and predicaments any different from those of Job, Jonah and your mother? Do you not know, *Those who suffer he rescues through suffering, and teaches them by the discipline of affliction?*[6] Is it not so, that like these three and many others, salvation was their faith?" Religion asked.

Language replied, "So, I suppose now you would have it that the phrase, *I am who I am*, is sacred and not allowed to be used by anyone else. What's more, all of this hangs on a statement by Moses that God told him this. Who's to say Moses didn't just come up with this on his own and then decide that it sounded like something that Jehovah should say, as our visitor suggested earlier?"

"Surely, you will rot in hell-fire and be damned forever!" RELIGION exclaimed.

"Yes, and who are you, LANGUAGE, to speak against the Almighty, anyway?" PAROCHIALITY said. I think FAITH and RELIGION have it about right. If you and EPISTEMOLOGY had your way, everything would be up for grabs and no one would know what anything means!"

At all of this Kyle could no longer contain himself and addressing the group said, "I've never seen such a charade or heard so much garbage in all my life. Besides, what is going on here? This is supposed to be the section of the Bible on *The Tower of Babel*, when instead each of you is vying for advantage

---

6   Job, Verses, 36:15, New English Bible, Oxford Study Edition.

and we've gone around in circular arguments that look like they could go on forever. What a place!"

"As a visitor you've acquitted yourself quite well," GOD said. "Whenever someone drops by, like yourself, we go round and round with this confusion in recognition of the *Tower* and the intention as spelled out in the 'Good Book', *Genesis, 11:1-9*. After all, we are *words* in the book, *Words in Modern Interpretations of the Biblical Literature*. So whenever we get a visitor, we are obligated to re-create the confusion as outlined in the *Tower* story."

"Well you've done one hell of a job," Kyle replied, angrily, feeling duped.

"I submit that you really should feel enlightened! While you may not have heard all the arguments that swirl around such ideas suggested by the *Tower*, you certainly should at least admit that you now go forth with greater knowledge and a better sense of the confusion that abounds in the world. Language can obfuscate as easily as illuminate any given subject. It's the minds of men and women who cause all the turmoil in the world," ENLIGHTENMENT said.

"Yeah, no kidding. I've lived with it all my life," Kyle said.

ENLIGHTENMENT went on, "Some people attribute all great and good things to the Lord, some people attribute all bad things to a devil, an instrument of evil; but thankfully some people have come to realize there is no intentionally good or bad in the world, except as acts or behaviors of people who choose to act in one manner or the other, either for good or bad. This is not to say that terrible things don't happen, like plagues, earthquakes, and floods, etc. But they, of course, are not the intentional acts of people!"

"Thank you all, but my God! I've had enough! I'm out of here," Kyle said as he got up to leave.

"Sit down!" GOD commanded. "You don't get off that easily. I have a little story to tell. I myself continue to wonder, as the good book says,

What doth it profit a man if he shall gain the world and lose his own soul?" [7]

"It is our practice here to send visitors forth with a little something for their effort that is over and above the material world that you come from, a little something to nourish the spirit, as it were."

"Recently, when I had some spare time, I had an experience that I think will likely enhance your experience in the *Land of Shinar*, where the *tower* stood. So, I beg your indulgence. Of course, almost everywhere I go I am paid great deference. I know I really do get away with murder sometimes. Lord knows enough others have done so using my name. So saying, I had the good fortune to find a local philosophy class that was right up my alley, and I hardly could contain myself when I dropped in and saw that on the blackboard behind the professor was written, 'Subject for Discussion Today: The God of Our Fathers is Dead!'"

"Apparently, I dropped in just as a student was responding to the professor's question, 'Is this the best of all possible worlds?'"

"The student said, 'I believe that the foundation for the argument by Leibniz that this is the best of all possible worlds is really no longer viable. Therefore, I believe, right now, we can easily argue that this is the only world we have, or any real possibility of having, so good or bad it is therefore the best of all

---

[7]   Paul, I Corinthians, 10:13, KJV

possible worlds, or the worst, of all possible worlds...since the same parameters apply in either case.'"

"The professor, briefly chagrined, addressed the student, 'Don't you think that's a rather superficial argument? I'd like to hear what would constitute the best, or worst, possible worlds, as the case may be. Does one triumph over the other? What is the likelihood of making a better world, or is our world doomed to self-destruct, due to man-made elements, like pollution, nuclear war, terrorism, plagues, over-population, etc., not to mention, of course, the ugly willful acts of man himself? And, of course, we must consider this with the possible existence of a supreme being—a creator, if you please, since the larger question of the best world begs the question, if there is a creator, then why have we inherited the world we have, or maybe it answers the question that because of all the confusion and destructive forces that there is no evidence for a creator.'"

"Another student piped up saying, 'While we know the Biblical stories offer great insight in the history of our early ancestors, and we also know science has exposed all the Biblical stories of creation as myths, used to explain people's cosmology and the origins of their creation stories, and we also know that there is virtually no scientific evidence for the existence of a God as our early ancestors envisioned him. At the same time, we cannot say with any certainty that there isn't a divine creator of the universe either.'"

"This last student had a rather remarkable story and this is where her story really begins. I call it, perhaps mistakenly:

CLOSE TO HEAVEN

The young woman went on to say, I'd like to present a little different view to address these issues. When I was a little girl I loved to sit with my grandfather who would tell me many stories and answer my

120

questions about life and the reason for being. He told me about the horrible times he had known in eastern Europe during the 1930s, seeing his friends and neighbors often times hauled away, only later to find they had gone to the death camps. Other times he saw neighbors being summarily tortured and shot. He said he could find no sane rationale for what was happening all around him. Consequently, he joined the resistance and fought the Nazi regime. But this was not an easy choice for Grandfather. He told me that sometimes he participated in terrible things for the greater good of *defeating the Nazis*! He would often say when reflecting, "Ayala, all men have the capacity for evil!"

Later Grandfather emigrated to the United States, where he saw people rejected just because of their beliefs and national origins. He used to wonder aloud, saying, "How in this great democracy could such unjust actions take place?"

Sometimes he would go on, "What is that Statue doing in New York harbor?" And then he'd recite the lines he knew by heart, from Emma Lazarus' poem, *The New Colossus*, on the plaque attached to Lady Liberty,

> Give me your tired, your poor,
> Your huddled masses yearning to breathe free,
> The wretched refuse of your teeming shore.
> Send these, the homeless, tempest-tost to me,
> I lift my lamp beside the golden door!

Grandfather could recite the whole poem from memory, but this was the part that he loved and when he did recite it, tears would come to his eyes.

On one of these occasions I asked him, "Why, Grampa, how does this happen, when everyone is supposed to be treated the same?"

"People don't always do what they should do," Grandfather said. "Sometimes they're selfish or lazy and sometimes they act out of hate and do bad things! So maybe they don't like somebody because of who he is, or where he comes from; so, they do what they think is right and not what they're supposed to do, if they can get away with it. I'm sorry to have to say, Ayala, that's just very wrong! Also, others may just stand by and let bad and unfair things happen for any number of reasons."

When talking about this unfairness and awful treatment of others, Grandfather then could get so caught up in this line of talk that he couldn't stop himself. One time I remember him mentioning the lynching of blacks in the South of the United States and how mobs would do horrible things and how others, who didn't actually participate, stood by as spectators and watched.

This time I particularly remember him saying, "Ayala, this is the evil that men and women sometimes do to one another! It is only within ourselves that we must find the inner conviction and courage to stand up against these awful things."

Grandfather became a very successful merchant on the Lower East Side in New York City. He was involved in many community efforts to improve the lives of those in his community. Though most were Jewish, some were not – he did not discriminate. He helped all who came to him for assistance, sometimes reaching into his own pocket.

I remember asking Grandfather how such awful things could be going on while others were enjoying seemingly happy lives.

He replied, "Life is not fair, Ayala! Each person must do the best they can within the circumstances that are handed to them. Sadly, there are places in our world where life is just plain hell! Then there are other places where life is good and people are happy to be alive. While mankind has caused most of the misery brought on in our world, we cannot forget that nature has also brought cataclysmic events on our planet as well!"

"How can God do this to people, Grandpa?" I asked.

"For those living in places where abject misery abounds, it would seem there is no God, though many may cling to their beliefs in spite of their misery! For those enjoying life, they may attribute their well-being to a just and loving God. But for those of us who reflect on the situation of our world in general, often times including our own personal experiences, there is little objective reason to believe that the *God of Our Fathers* governs in the affairs of mankind. The abundant information in our time dispels any myths or basis for such faith," Grandfather said.

"Is there no God at all?" I asked him.

"I certainly can't answer that," Grandfather said, "but I must hasten to add that no one, as far as I know, has proven that there is *no* divine presence in the universe either. So we are left in the quandary that there is no God as we have known him in the past, or if there is a divine presence, we have no knowledge of its workings or intentions."

"Does that mean when we die that's the end of us, that we don't go on after death?" I asked.

"Ah, that is the age-old question," Grandfather replied. "For me, I can only say, I don't know and I do wonder, does it really matter? I've had a full and wonderful life. Do I really want to go on to the Elysian Fields and for what, what would I do there – listen to the harps all the time and dream of my days in earthly bliss? No, Ayala, this question has no answer, at least not for me. What's more if there is something afterwards, then that will be a totally new experience. Why would I have any idea of what that all might be? I certainly haven't heard anything in this world that makes me want to go to the proverbial *hereafter!*"

"Then what's the purpose of it all? Why are we here, Grandpa?" I asked.

"I surely don't know the answer to these questions either," he replied. "But, while we are here I believe we must assert ourselves to do the best we can to improve our lives and those of our fellow human beings. We only have this one world that we know of, and it is in sore need of all the help it can get. It is up to each of us who cares to do as much as each of us is able to help save our planet and to promote a community for the greater good of all who inhabit it," Grandfather said. Then he continued, "Is this world perfect? No, far from it! But for me I've found my place and it is close enough to Heaven for me."

Addressing Kyle, GOD said, "Now, my son, you may go. But, I suggest that you take this parable to heart and promote good will and good deeds wherever you go. For the soul of a man is really priceless and, in my humble opinion, the one lesson you should take from your visit here today is that there is more than enough discord and misery in the world to go around. The question is, do you want to lay up earthly stores for an end that separates you from the world of material possessions, or do you want to do things that sustain yourself and the lives of others as an intrinsic measure of self-worth and personal value, things that will be sorely missed when you have departed. Remember, *It is easier for a camel to go through the eye of a needle than for a rich man to enter the kingdom of Heaven!*"[8]

"That's all interesting and certainly food for thought, but it surely doesn't address my problem of being stuck in Limbo. When is God going to offer me the gift of faith and free me from this unholy bondage?" Kyle said.

Then he got up, thanked everyone for their time, and walked out the door, back into the *Table of Contents*. Only then did he, again, remember that he could just exit the program by using the handholds and pressing the exit button.

"God, let me get out of here! The 'eye of a needle' be damned, I'd a hell of lot rather die rich than poor and I'd sure hate to get lost in this book!" he thought as he pushed the button that he thought would end the program he was in.

---

[8]   Matthew, Verses, 19:24, KJV.

GETTING THE PICTURE

There was a whirling and dizzying display before Kyle found himself staring at another doorway with the inscription, *A Dialog from the Painter's Palette: Table of Contents*.

"What the hell is going on? Something must be wrong with this application," he thought, without realizing he still had his helmet on. Quickly grabbing the handholds, he walked through the doorway and found himself in another room where he was surrounded with more doors. The first door on his immediate left had the inscription, *Forums: Introduction to Art and Art History*.

"I guess I'll just do like Dad said and just get on with it and stop fighting this world. Besides, what do I have to lose? So, *intro to art* – might as well start at the beginning," he thought, as he entered the room.

Immediately, upon entering, he was facing a desk with a sign: *Painting, Drawing and Sculpting Conference: Registration*. Words were moving forward to sign in, picking up agenda packets and moving off. As Kyle's turn in line came, an agent came up and asked, "Are you already registered and are you a member or visitor?"

"I'm not registered and I'm a visitor too, I guess."

"Please sign up here," the agent said, handing him a clipboard with a registration-sign-in sheet, with two columns, Name and Occupation.

As Kyle looked at the sheet he could see the entries on the line above where he was about to sign in; under Name was the word *Easel* and under Occupation was the word *Noun*. Seeing this, Kyle entered *I* for Name and *Pronoun* for occupation. The agent then printed off his nametag, with the word *Visitor* at top in red and his name and occupation below in blue, and put it in a lanyard.

Moving off and looking around, he found himself in a large auditorium with all these things running around that looked like toothpaste tubes, but each one a different color – their lanyards hanging off of them. Looking around he could see other objects. Some looked like painters' palettes, others looked like brushes, easels and other painting, drawing and sculpting paraphernalia. As he continued looking around, he could see the room was filling with all these objects. On the stage, he could see several tubes that stood out because of their larger size, each one a different primary or secondary color. Other objects were also present on the stage, and as best as Kyle could tell they were representative of some of the different groups in the auditorium.

Kyle asked OCHER, a tube standing nearby, what was going on.

"You're lucky," he said, "you're here for the opening session, where some of the major concerns of the association will be discussed. Afterwards, you can find focus groups in the breakout rooms surrounding this meeting hall."

Just as OCHER was about to say something more, there was a banging of the gavel and the primary color, RED was calling the assembly to order.

"My friends, it gives me great pleasure to see such a gay and colorful group assembled here today. It is indeed an auspicious occasion when we convene with such a diverse group, all of whom help to express the artistic dimensions of the world. Generally speaking, of course, art is almost universally recognized as the highest form of expression. I know it's a cliché, but don't we all know that *a picture's worth a thousand words*?"

At this the audience broke out in thunderous applause.

RED raised his hands to calm the applause, saying, "Thank you, thank you!" He then went on, "I must hasten to add that we must also include sculpture, photography, creative writing, poetry and the other modern forms of artistic expression as also expanding communication exponentially! Having been selected as the moderator of today's session, I want to outline some of the topics up for discussion today, and, of course, we will ask for additional topics from the audience, but first I want to introduce our esteemed panel. On my far right is MALLET, representing sculpture; next to him is No. 12 Filbert BRUSH, known to everyone around here as just the BRUSH. Both EASEL and PALETTE are on my immediate right, representing art accessories; to my left are YELLOW, GREEN and BLUE, who, along with myself, represent colors; lastly, but certainly not least, next to the colors, is our distinguished colleague, WORD for the Writers Guild, whom I may also add will be in attendance at the Forum for the Performing Arts on the other side of this hall."

Kyle was totally taken aback. Yes, there he was, his new friend, WORD! But Kyle's reverie was interrupted.

RED, lifting his arms in front of him in a welcoming gesture and looking out to the audience, continued, "I'd like to now call for any additional topics that are of special concern to our members."

At this, an object raised his hand and RED called for No. 2 PENCIL to stand saying, "What is your topic PENCIL?"

"We, that is myself, CHARCOAL, PEN and INK and all our associates that work on cartoons are really disgusted at the tone that some of our work has set in national as well as international forums. We're disgusted at the incendiary and inflammatory nature of these creations. We strongly feel that no medium has the unfettered right to insult, defame and mock others' beliefs, particularly those of a religious nature," PENCIL exclaimed.

"Very good! *Where do We Draw the Line*, so noted! Any other topics for discussion?" Red asked.

A hand shot up in the back of the room. Kyle gasped! He was amazed to see it was THOUGHT.

"I know it's been brought up before, but I continue to wonder why painting often includes words. Linguists in my community are concerned with this unbridled use of this form of mixed media. I have to say we were all appalled with some of the paintings by a well-known French painter. After all, if a painting is worth a thousand words, isn't it a contradiction to think that you then have to explain it?" THOUGHT questioned aloud.

"Please, not that old saw again!" RED exclaimed. "I'm afraid it's an accepted art form. Now I will admit there was a bit of confusion when we were forced last year to examine the issue of a drawing of a piece of charcoal containing the caption *This Is Not a Piece of Charcoal*, but, if you remember, the committee ruled that it too qualified as mixed-media art!"

At this, WORD interjected from the stage.

"Well, can't we at least assign it to a specific category?"

"So one work may qualify as Surrealism, another as Modern. Wouldn't that just be splitting hairs? After all, this group fully supports unfettered expression! I think that kind of definition would just be painting ourselves into a corner," RED said.

"Any other topics?" RED called to the audience.

A hand, raised by a roll of canvas, brought immediate recognition by RED.

"I, myself, ACADEMY-BOARD and WOOD-PANEL, would like the committee to settle the question, once and for all, regarding the origins of the phrase *off the wall*. We believe this phrase came about when painting and art moved from being adornments in religions institutions as frescos and huge framed paintings permanently attached to their respective surfaces to smaller portable framed paintings that are often used as decorative pieces, moving from one location to another as personal taste dictates. However, we can find no mention of this term with respect to the antecedents of modern paintings. We find the current interpretations of *off the wall*, such as bizarre, eccentric, gonzo, outlandish, etc., to be very offensive," CANVAS said.

"What do you think this is? Framing a definition for *off the wall*, so you think we're revisionists? It's this very same type of question that deflects us from our primary purpose. In fact, this question itself is a perfect example of *off the wall*! I think it is ludicrous, if not bizarre and outlandish to boot!" RED stated, and, trying to regain his composure, he asked if there were any more suggested topics.

No further topics from the audience were offered.

Although taken with the proceedings so far, Kyle was really more interested in finding his way across the room to where THOUGHT was sitting. "Hi THOUGHT, good to see you."

"WORD and I spotted you when you came in and we were really surprised. We thought you'd be up to your eyeballs in Remedial Grammar by now," THOUGHT replied.

"It's a long story!" Kyle exclaimed. "I thought you and WORD had other business to attend to."

"Well, we did and actually this conference is part of our other business as you could, no doubt, tell from my earlier question and WORD's place up with the honchos." He was about to go on, but RED had started talking again.

"Our other topics for today's forum include trying to better delineate the differences between Commercial Art and art for art's sake; grave-stone rubbings (do these qualify as art?); the purpose of reproductions and the digital revolution."

RED continued, "As the highpoint of our conference and to kick things off, as we do every session, we will be asking visitors to come up and tell us a little bit about themselves and present a creation in keeping with their occupation or vocation."

Kyle shuddered, praying that they not call on him, but at the same time his mind was racing to think of something he could come up with.

Just then RED announced, "I'd like call on a visitor and a new 'I', otherwise called Kyle Wilson, to come up to present himself and tell us about his creative work."

Kyle grew flush with embarrassment. Tentatively and awkwardly, he rose from his chair and walked to the podium. With an equal amount of diffidence, he started.

"Thank you, RED. Good afternoon fellow words. In a large sense, I feel myself an interloper, since I find myself here totally out of happenstance. In other words, I'm not here out of choice, but out of some caprice of fate or nature. That being the case, let me at least give you an overview. Prior to arriving here, I have been a supervisory librarian at a University Library in New Hampshire. Recently, however, I've found myself deeply enmeshed in letters, words and other various realms, where to a large extent, I've been forced to reengage with my recent and distant past. Very soon, after finding myself in an altered state, I discovered I have been the victim of an auto accident that resulted in a serious head injury and a coma. Subsequent seizures followed, resulting in a determination of being almost braindead. During the development of this situation, I initially found myself in a Land of Letters, where I was reminded of my early childhood, my difficulty with spelling, subsequent anxiety and trauma, then the loss of my mother and the forced move to begin a new family life with her birth family."

"Later, in the Land of Words and other realms, I was forced to accept my inadequacy with English grammar. All this while, I was on various occasions made privy to the clinical diagnosis and medical status of my current mental state. These medical interludes left me with the distinct impression that my fate and any possibility of recovery will be through divine providence or some mysterious ability on my part. At least, that is the conclusion of the doctors, who have attended me so far. What I'm beginning to learn is that my current environment and social milieu will likely decide my fate. At least that is the conclusion that I have come to, after associations in these new realms and a recent meeting with my father."

"A later meeting with my mother only reinforced my notion that I lack a sustaining faith that would help me to become self-possessed, whole and restored to good health."

"Of course, this doesn't tell the whole story. One major aspect of growing up was my turn to alcohol to cope with the issues in my life and to deal with my inadequacy and my personal problems. Thus, began my descent into full-blown addiction. Through psychotherapy and a 12-step program I was able to put the 'plug in the jug', so to speak. However, with these recent events and experiences in the Land of Letters, Land of Words and other realms, I see the place of addiction, in my life, more clearly than ever."

"Addiction was just a symptom of my inability to cope. It afforded me a way of avoiding responsibility for my actions, only forestalling the inevitable anxiety that surrounded attempts at engagement in life. Ultimately, it was fear that drove me to drink – fear of failure; fear of rejection and pervasive low self-esteem. To a large extent I managed to see these boogeymen for what they were and I slowly built a wholesome self-image, engaged in healthy personal relationships and went on to a gainful career."

"Now, with these new and recent experiences, I see the place of addiction in proper perspective. In the end, I can see that my father and mother found their personal recipes for living. My recent engagements with them offers me great insight adding to the quality and wellbeing of my life, if I ever manage to escape my current predicament."

"Art and artistic expression have certainly been a unique and elevating factor in my life that, to some extent, carried me through my years of personal struggle. On the subject of creativity, in spite of my recent predicament, I'm honored to be here with a group that truly knows the importance of art. All of us know that regimes, dictators and tyrants rise and fall as our world turns, but art, alone, endures!"

"Otherwise, at first and really throughout my time in these new worlds, I found myself in self-reflection – what life's all about and, generally, how am I to cope? Fortunately, in the form of poetry, the muse continues to speak to me through the greatest of mediums, the reflexive process that we call life. Thus, I share with you a new poem I've just conceived."

NEW BEGINNINGS

When early on, I was thrust into this fray,
I thought and fought in quite a different way.

In my old world of beliefs and manners and how I used to live,
and with calls to change that former life, in I could not give.

Accept what comes your way, was father's sage prescription.
Instead, the course of years' long habits was implacable addiction.

From mother, unshakeable faith, example of a moral essence.
I scoffed and said, if God exists, let him bestow acceptance.

Now confronted with worlds anew, at my wits' end,
'how to live' escapes me, as to the maelstrom I descend.

Perhaps father and mother, in their ways, knew the sober truth.
I battle now for faith, acceptance, and life itself, absent any proof.

For in these strange new realms, as in daily life, I have but little choice.
To save my very being, I give up my old ways and search to find my voice.

There were resounding rounds of applause, with shouts of 'bravo', as RED stepped back to the podium, saying, "Thank you so much Kyle, that was wonderful! This was truly art in its best sense, a spontaneous, sincere expression! Your story is really a metaphor for the story of art in general, and it typifies the journey of many an artist."

RED then asked, "Are there any questions from the audience?"

A hand shot up, it was CANVAS, "While I know writing falls within the bounds of our conference, I thought we focused on *Painting, Drawing and Sculpting*, as the conference billing says, so why are we talking about a writer-poet?"

RED, obviously displeased by the question, retorted, "Really, CANVAS, I didn't think I'd ever have to paint the picture for you! Kyle's story is about a man, who is struggling to find his muse. Just how graphic do you expect an example to be? In my mind, I could have just as easily told you the story of Van Gogh, but this story is just more immediate and I thought it would be very timely and appropriate, so may I suggest and even emphasize that you draw whatever conclusions you like! Furthermore, your question certainly falls well within the real definition of *off the wall* that you asked about earlier, something that I hope you'll take as constructive criticism, an experience that you can draw on later in life. After all, everything isn't always drawn on canvas!"

Kyle, obviously shaken by the question, went back to his seat.

"We'll now take up the topics for discussion. Please hold any questions until the panel has completed discussing the particular topic."

RED then turned to the Panel, now all seated in back of a long rectangular table, and asked, *"Where do We Draw the Line,* when it comes to satire and mocking religions and other sensitive, cultural issues?"

MALLET, the first to speak, said, "Obviously, these derogatory cartoons, while not chiseled in stone, have had a very deleterious effect on some cultures and have also had very serious consequences for some individuals. When I was growing up as a young lad, it was often said one man's rights existed as far as the next man's nose. Since we cannot legislate against the things that are allowed as free speech in our constitution, it is up to each individual to exercise a certain amount of personal restraint when dealing with sensitive topics. I believe that this group should come up with a statement of purpose for all who practice art. We might, for instance, call it the *Golden Rule of Art*, for example, sing about, write about, paint or sculpt others as you would have them render you."

"Excellent idea! I make a motion, as an action of this committee, that we accept MALLET'S suggested *Golden Rule of Art* as a statement of principle in the organizational precepts of our organization," the BRUSH said. "We just can't go on sweeping this issue under the carpet, so to speak, as we have so many times in the past. After all, if you want to go on making those kinds of derogatory comments and creating mocking images, you should do so at your own peril and be prepared to suffer the consequences. I submit that we should no longer sanction such creations as art, and we will give no quarter to such perpetrators in the future!"

"Are we then to deny as art works such as *Fountain*, by Marcel Duchamp, which is now an accepted part of his oeuvre?" YELLOW asked.

"Look, it may be fine china, but I certainly don't find it as representative of 'fine art'!" MALLET responded. After all, what's illuminating or imaginative about an upside-down urinal? If that's art, then why not daub it with a little excrement to add to its creative dimensions, adding an olfactory dimension to the work?"

I make a motion that we accept the *Golden Rule of Art* as a statement of principle in the organizational precepts of our organization, just as MALLET has suggested and the BRUSH has moved," EASEL said.

"We'll have a vote now with a show of hands. All those in favor of the proposed statement?" RED asked.

Only YELLOW refused to vote for the new measure. "The new statement, as outlined, is now accepted and will henceforth be included in our organizational precepts," RED said.

"For our second topic we move to 'delineating the difference between commercial art and art for art's sake.' Does any one of our panel members want to open the discussion?" RED asked.

"This topic is certainly apropos to the times we live in, when everyone is trying to turn a buck and get rich," PALETTE said.

"What do you think? Artists don't need to eat?" the BRUSH said.

"It would be nice if it really were that simple, but we all know it's far more complicated than that. In our own time, we've seen artist's estates spring up as manufacturing centers for famous artists, reproducing their works on all kinds of objects, not to mention prints of varying quality and of every size, as well as books and pamphlets. Some of these master artists would turn over in their graves if they could only see the unbridled greed attached to their works," PALETTE replied.

"Oh, so you think those who struggled so hard for recognition in the past would now turn up their noses and spurn the comforting flow of cash into their coffers? I hardly think so!" BLUE said.

"Well, that's true, but generally don't we think of commercial art as being associated with advertising? I say art is usually considered to be the product or products of creativity and imagination, in any number of forms. It's easy to say that commercial art is just a subset of the all-encompassing term, art, as we know it," BRUSH said.

"I think it's pretty clear that there are artists and then there are artists; those who struggle to express their thoughts and passions, and those who merely exploit their own talent as a means to turning a buck. Whether someone turns a buck or not is hardly the determining factor as to whether art is of a rare quality or is a general, run-of-the-mill expression. If one can turn a buck while practicing a particular art form, then that would, at the very least, indicate there is some appeal to someone's creations. This also begs the question, is one's art really diminished if they find a ready cash market for their inspirations?" EASEL queried.

"Can we not at the least acknowledge that, in general, art is an expression of one's subjective thoughts and feelings, and whether it is of great or little value doesn't diminish the fact that it constitutes art? Whether any particular art is in demand or is highly desirable is a wholly different matter. As for commercial art, well, as we've already said, it's primarily advertising, which is denoted by its very description in the first place," YELLOW added.

At this point a lone voice yelled out from the audience. G-CLEF, waiting to attend the Performing Arts Conference, spoke up, "Should we not recognize and at least sing the praises of all the unsung heroes and heroines of art, who put their mediums before all other considerations? I can, for instance, think of no better example of the artist who works and lives an ignoble life than that of the now celebrated Vincent van Gogh!"

And then G-CLEF launched into song,

> "On an easel, I paint my heart,
> No one cares that it was art.
> Where, oh where does the painter go?
> In search of acclaim, he'll never know…"

"Stop!" RED yelled, "I think we've examined this topic enough to say that further discussion at this time is not called for."

"As to our next topic, 'grave-stone rubbings, do these qualify as art'?" RED asked.

"I don't really have a dog in this fight and it's such a moribund topic. I have to say I don't think they should qualify as art, but maybe they could qualify as copies of art, depending, of course, on the nature of the reproduction. After all, I've seen some fantastic rubbings, such as images of knights and ladies from some old artistic tombstones," PALETTE said.

"But it does take a certain amount of skill to execute a good rubbing, not to mention selecting stones that have great appeal because of some unusual feature that they possess. I say they constitute art," BLUE said.

RED turned to the group, "Well, are they or are they not art?" he asked.

By a show of hands, it was almost unanimous that they should be considered art.

"Now last, the purpose of reproductions and the digital revolution," RED announced.

"Aside from being an income stream, reproductions are probably the main means of disseminating art. And the digital revolution, well, that certainly is one of the biggest vehicles ever, in the history of the world, for disseminating art or anything else!" YELLOW said.

"Of course, you can also search for art and art reproductions on the web as well as purchase almost anything you desire," PALETTE added. He continued, "The Internet has opened up a whole new world, providing access to a myriad of things and information about almost anything. However, I hasten to add, the digital age has also added new dimensions not only to printing, but, more importantly, to the art world, as it offers new approaches to color, something I can personally testify to. As most of you probably know, the new age has given birth to colors you would have never dreamed of before the electronic age. Adding to these new dimensions are, of course, software graphic programs that are bound to enhance the technical prowess of almost any artist."

GREEN, who had been quiet, said, "I don't see any reason for splitting hairs on the issue of color and where it comes from! We all know that the hues are different to everyone. Color is pretty much a subjective experience, and some viewers may be far off the mark, seeing distorted views. This is only to say that sights, while colorful, may be far off the mark from what was the artist's intention, in the mind's eye, so to speak. Some other viewers literally can't even distinguish between any colors other than BLACK and WHITE. Naturally, I do try to always present myself in the best light; in fact, so much so that others are often very envious," GREEN said. "And besides I can't be responsible for the experiences of every Tom, Dick and Harry!"

"That's enough," RED interrupted, adding, "We don't need to add any more ambiguity to a subject that's already murky enough. I think I speak for most of us here when I say that it's been too long a habit of artists to hold their cards a little too close, keeping us all guessing. I believe it's time we look behind the painter's canvas to see where the likes of that enigmatic smile of the Mona Lisa resides. Is it in the particular stroke of a brush, or perhaps it lurks just below the surface in a form of pentimento? I'm hoping our efforts will lead to a greater openness in the art world and that there is a move away from the obscurantism of the past."

RED then said, "This concludes our plenary session. Please do check the breakout rooms around this hall for workshops and specialty sessions. I would also like to call everyone's attention to the Performing Arts Conference in the adjoining hall. That begins in just about an hour."

By this point WORD had joined THOUGHT and Kyle.

Kyle asked, "What are you two up to now? I was thinking of looking around a bit."

"Yeah, that sounds okay for a little while," WORD replied. "We've got a little time on our hands, so why not. What do you say, THOUGHT?"

"Good deal," he replied.

As the three walked around the hall, Kyle saw a sign, *Poets Corner*. "Can we take a look?" he asked.

His companions both nodded in assent and the three went in.

"I had no idea you had the gift. I've always loved poetry," WORD said. "Words are so often turned on their heads, so to speak, to give precise meanings of thoughts and feelings. Of course, every poet is constrained by grammar and rhythmic schemes. Oh, there is free verse, but that lyrical quality has to shine through if a poem's going to work at all. Naturally, meaning is a big part of it too. A little doggerel is acceptable if it's an obvious intention of the given poet."

"That's all true, but it's the depth of thought to express an idea or emotion that touches us in a special way, much like music does in a very visceral sense," THOUGHT added.

At that moment, a light went on at one of the little mini stages nearby and an object that looked just like a prism stepped up to the podium and started speaking, "Good afternoon everyone. For those of you who don't know me, I'm UNIQUE! Oh, you might say I'm a bit of a philosopher, but a unique one, none the less. I've been a poet for a number of years now and that's because the easiest way to understand me is through my poetry. That's at least partly true because by my very nature it's not easy to see through me. I know everything looks distorted that way, but I think for those who really want to know me, it forces them to read my poems."

"I had an interesting experience the other day. As I was grooming one recent morning, I had one of those mirror moments, and I must admit I was overcome with a tremendous sense of curiosity about who I am. Thereupon I set to work on this poem that may seem a bit remote for one such as myself, but I ask each of you to empathize and put yourself in my place and then ask yourself, what poem would you write? Well, my friends, that is the poem that I am going to read today. I call it,

I AM

In infancy, I was a mewling tot.
I knew not whence I came,
nor what would be my lot.

Both parents did gaga over me.
I did cry and coo,
to fill their hearts with glee.

Then terrible twos did come.
I, an innocent little devil,
did test their love in sum.

Next I struggled to be a little man.
Parents were sure to laugh and coddle,
while my future they did plan.

At five I was striking out in search of friends.
Mom and dad in my footsteps,
steering as they could, but followed to all ends.

Two years later, me getting my ideas,
they found no fault in anything I said.
I was to have no peers.

As a teen, I surely tried them to extreme.
They, confused, did go the extra mile,
praying only that I not go off the beam.

As older teen, I was full of big ideas.
They soldiered on at every turn.
With boundless love, I mastered many fears.

College years would prove a way to my own life.
They held true, for the path I took.
The world is tough, they said, and pitfalls they are rife.

A budding philosopher, the road I chose was rough.
Parents indulged my many different thoughts.
I would find myself by God, however hard or tough.

When last I arrived in my profession, with my own bran',
parents gone, I asked myself who I was.
I did not like Descartes' idea, "I think, therefore I am."

Descartes' idea be damned, my ambitions are to soar.
An individual first, then I think, therefore I am who I am.
A philosopher, I was sure, is so much more.

And now I become a poet and at peace.
I find what matters most in this old world,
is to enjoy the life I have before I cease!"

"Bravo, bravo," WORD yelled, along with the applause of many others.

"Holy cow!" Kyle, cried, "Talk about someone stealing your thunder, that should have been my poem!"

"Don't beat on yourself, you'll get there," THOUGHT said.

"Yeah, right. *I am who I am*, and I wonder just who the hell that is? In this place, I'm still thinking about that one, but maybe I'm also beginning to get a little taste of acceptance," Kyle said.

UNIQUE asked, "Any questions or thoughts?"

A question arose from a word in the back of the audience, "Don't you feel that you've taken some liberties using that last stanza?"

"Well perhaps, but first please tell us who you are," UNIQUE said.

"LICENSE, at your service," the word replied. "I hope you know that you can only carry this poetic thing just so far."

"Something in particular about this particular poem that bothers you?" UNIQUE asked.

"Well it's just that I find many of you poets are just dying to get in the last word. Why don't you just leave that last stanza off and acknowledge you're UNIQUE. I mean I'm all for poetic license, but give me a break!" LICENSE said.

"Well, I just feel that in life, death is always with us. We can't escape it and when we're actually dead, well what can you say then?" UNIQUE replied. "Now I'm getting on in years, with many thoughts that go far beyond my ego. Yes, I am who I am, but I'm also so much more. My heart aches to touch the world in a way that transcends my corporeal self. Unfettered poetry seems the perfect vehicle for that and if you have a problem with it, well, revoke my license or whatever it is you do. If I have to I'll write fugitive poetry. At this stage, what have I got to lose?"

Just then THOUGHT turned to WORD and said, "Hey, we better be going, otherwise we'll be late." With that, Kyle joined in, and the three of them walked back out into the hall.

WORD then said to Kyle, "Look, we have some other commitments, so you can go along and hopefully get back into Remedial Grammar."

PLAYING FOR KEEPS

After his friends left, Kyle decided to go across the hall and drop in on the *Performing Arts Conference*. He was surprised to see a theatrical stage with a large sign, *Drama and the Theatre of Life*, above the curtains.

The hall, in the form of a theatre, was rapidly filling with all kinds of objects and some items were also gathering on the stage.

As Kyle took his seat, he noticed a small pamphlet that he quickly realized was a program guide. Inside was outlined the events with opening remarks by none other than MUSIC. The highlight listed in the program guide was the play, *Maturity, What's That?*

After taking his seat, Kyle had barely finished reading the program, when MUSIC, who looked like a Baton, was at the podium, banging a gavel and calling the conference to order.

"A warm welcome to all! We're here tonight with fellow musicians, directors, conductors, actors, singers, stage-experts, script writers, and many other special guests. I truly am pleased to see you here tonight."

"We have a great program planned today. Unlike our uptight colleagues in the visual arts across the hall, we're a little less tightly wrapped. At the risk of digressing, I've often wondered if it's because of the permanent form of their art, that I really do admire, that they seem to think they're a little better than the rest of us. But in my mind, I think it's the performing arts that really transcend, and I think they more than even the score; pardon the pun. True to this philosophy, you won't be finding any lengthy dialectic trying to resolve this or that point in our program, as that seldom resolves anything! You see, in music and all the performing arts, it's really the experience that counts. Sure, some, musicians, in particular, do intellectually understand performance art, like music and drama, but by far, and more importantly, it's the experience and the memories that the audience walks away with that really matters. Through the performance one can be transformed, enlightened or motivated to act in some particular fashion. In sum, who cannot recall a good belly laugh as well as a concealed tear or two, at some performance or other."

"Speaking of performances that stir one's emotions in one way or another, and in keeping with our performance today, I'm reminded of the times I attended a few of the great symphonies, probably Beethoven or Mahler, summer performances, at an open-air theatre in the Berkshires, an area that adjoins the Catskills."

"Washington Irving made this area famous with his tale *Rip Van Winkle*, the obverse of any ideal concerning maturity, the subject of our play today, but a lesson in maturity all the same. This story came to mind today as I thought about this subject and the capricious nature of life that impinges on us all, at one time or another. It is not without a touch of irony that the story would come to me now. At that theatre in the Berkshires, deafening thunderstorms always seemed to show up. We didn't know life without the storms on hot summer nights. It often was as though nature herself was not to be left out or outdone by these magnificent and vibrant symphonies. Certainly, any of the audience who knew the area's lore, during those crashing, dissonant crescendos of man and nature, could not help but conjure up memories of the tale of Rip and Henry Hudson's crew playing nine-pins, the purported cause of the spectacular thunder! In contrast to Rip, who ran away from life, our performance today is about coming to grips with one's life."

"It's called, *Maturity, What's That?* It's a play that shows one young man's struggle for maturity, but then begs the question, just exactly what is that, and how does one know if they've arrived at that questionable state? And, might I add, given the nature of our audience, it is a word play. We also want to welcome a special visitor, Mr. Kyle Wilson, who will be starring in the role of the TEENAGER. Kyle, please come on up."

Looking out to the audience, MUSIC said, "Please help me welcome Kyle Wilson!"

There was a loud clapping of hands.

Totally flummoxed, Kyle got up from his seat, blushing and confused, but he dutifully went up to the stage. After bowing and pretending to be honored by all the attention, he turned to MUSIC and, shouting over all the background noise, "What the hell is going on? Are you crazy? I have no idea of what this is all about, what I'm supposed to do, or even what the play is really about! And for that matter, I'm certainly no teenager either!"

"Oh, don't worry! The play works itself out. It's really a form of psychodrama, and you'll fall right into the part. You just say what's on your mind. That's what the part calls for, and you'll be ideal for the part!" MUSIC bantered.

"Jesus Christ! This place is crazy. How the hell did you even know I was here?" Kyle fumed.

Just then the lights went down, and MUSIC left the stage. Kyle was left on the stage by himself. The lights came back on and the curtain went up.

MATURITY, WHAT'S THAT?

Act I

Cast:

> TEENAGER, Kyle Wilson
> ADULT, a stick figure
> HOW, WHEN, WHERE, WHO, WHY and WHAT, all question marks with corresponding name tags
> REASON, thinking face emoji
> BUT, an emoji face with one eyebrow raised
> (showing skepticism, disbelief, or disapproval)

Scene I

In a small informal and relaxed classroom.

> **KYLE, talking to himself, unscripted, as he steps through the door with a sign at the top,** *Language, Self-Actualization and Maturity*:

> What the hell am I getting myself into now?
> **ADULT, close by hollers:** Careful, you're getting ahead of yourself.
> **KYLE, demanding:** What are you talking about and who are you anyway?
> **ADULT:** I'm your tutor and my name is ADULT. You really were getting ahead of yourself, you know.

KYLE: Who are you to say, and how do you know something like that?

ADULT: As I already said, I'm your tutor and I just happened to notice that you stepped through the door without even thinking about it. I'm afraid you're off to a very rocky start here!

KYLE: For Christ's sake, I'm not even through the door and you're on my back! Give me a break, will you? Who says I want you for a tutor or that I want any tutor for that matter?

ADULT: I heard that you're trying to be a little more accepting in life. You should know that passages in life are everything and certainly not to be taken lightly! You only get one tutor here and, true to most things in life, you best make the most of it.

KYLE: Look, I didn't ask to be here. I don't like this and I'm not going to do it.

ADULT: You don't have to like it, or even like me, for that matter, but you are going to do it.

KYLE: Who says? You can't make me do anything that I don't want to.

ADULT: I didn't realize I was getting someone quite so obtuse. You see, this is your life and one way or another you're going to grow and change. You'll change either with help and instruction or in spite of yourself. Then, of course, there's that little matter of becoming self-possessed that you talked about earlier in the art forum.

KYLE, sarcastically: Oh, and you're supposed to help me improve. So, what's up then, where do we start?

ADULT: Now, that's better, just be a little open to new things, and for starters don't balk at everything before you even know what's going on. Now, we know you grew up with problems and all, and look where that's gotten you.

KYLE angrily: Yeah, you got it. So, what?

ADULT: Well, look, let's not worry about it. I'm having a few friends over in a little bit. It's kind of a 'meet and greet', so don't be put off. They're a rather unusual crowd.

Enter HOW, WHEN and WHERE, they are followed in a short while by, WHO, WHY and WHAT.

ADULT: This is the family who has descended from a long line of questions.

ADULT then introduces REASON, who also just entered behind the questions: This, of course, is my most thought provoking friend, REASON!

All the guests are very effusive while drinks are being poured.

WHEN jokingly speaks to WHERE and KYLE is surprised: Oh, my God that really was the $64,000 question!

ADULT, tapping his glass with a utensil says: Gentlemen, I want to introduce my new understudy, Kyle Wilson.

WHAT, stretching out his hand in greeting to surprised KYLE: What brings you here?

KYLE: Some damned ruse! You don't want to know! The short answer, I guess, is Providence, that damned Eye, and I have no idea why. Otherwise, I overheard some jerk say I was in a persistent vegetative state, and I'm just hoping to recover, but why all these questions?

WHY, cutting KYLE off: Why you wonder? Ah yes, the preeminent question, if I do say so! Look, just why is it you're here? he probed.

HOW, before KYLE can answer: How is it you come to be here anyway?

WHERE, interrupting: Where were you before you got here?

WHEN, following: When did you arrive?

WHO, piles on: Who did you say you are again?

KYLE yelling and angry: Stop! For Christ's sake! What the hell is going on here? Next thing I know you guys will be bringing out the 'rack'.

ADULT: It's nothing personal. This is *Question Session*. You'll find after you've been here awhile, if you don't already know it, that one grows and develops by asking questions, not by blabbering. This little introduction, while a bit uncomfortable for you, was really just a way of demonstrating how one learns through questions. In keeping with our tradition of Self-Actualization I've asked our guest, WHY, to start us off with a little something to illustrate what I'm trying to show.

REASON, interrupting: Young man you're not alone; you have good reason to be upset. Endless questions drive everyone crazy! While we often hear, when someone prefaces a question with, 'I know this is a stupid question…' the reply frequently is 'there are no stupid questions'! However, in reality, there certainly are many stupid questions, but we must, up to a point, be indulgent enough, so the questioners eventually learn the folly of their ways, and ultimately know they had the answer right in hand, if they but reflected for a moment.

KYLE, interrupting: What the hell are you talking about, I haven't even asked a question, much less had a chance to get a word in edgewise!

ADULT, jumping in: Enough, everyone calm down! Young man, excuse me! You are here of your own free will, and I hope you will indulge us a bit, and you'll hopefully get the gist of self-actualization! After all, it is the question and the capacity to reason that helps one gain some degree of control and mastery over their own life, maybe even to becoming self-possessed. Now, I ask our friend, WHY, to take it away.

WHY, exuding an aura of self-confidence: I truly believe 'why' really is the preeminent question! It's not that I'm stuck on myself, or anything, but, of course, this further begs the question, why do I believe this? The answer is that there are very few things that happen in life that cannot be better understood by asking the simple question, *'why'*. Now when we look at that in the context of self-actualization, we very frequently must pursue any answer with the further question of *'why'*, and that resulting answer may, even yet again, require the further question of *'why'*, etc. That being said, I have a little story I'd like to tell. It's a story of a young man struggling to find himself in a world where he must confront both external obstacles and internal character flaws. So, everyone gather around.

(All players gather around WHY)

GROWING UP

"I suppose looking back I should have seen it all," Phillip Holland said to himself.

He remembered how it had started, back when he was relating his job woes to his friend Charlie, an employment counselor.

"I'm so damn sick of their bullshit!" Phil said. "You want to talk about mismanagement, don't go any farther than Uncle Sam. One hand never knows what the other is doing! And my boss, he couldn't find his ass with both hands if he was sitting on them!"

"Phil, get off it. You keep harping over the same old stuff. When are you going to come to grips with the here and now, and get on with your life?" Charlie challenged.

Phil also remembered he had just kept going on, "It isn't just my immediate boss. They're all assholes. If I want to keep my sanity, I've just got to bite the bullet and get out of that place. Add to that, what kind of social life do I have working that damn three to eleven shift. I barely have time for a few beers and then everything closes up, and I end up hanging around all the next morning, waiting to go to work."

And he remembered Charlie's rejoinder, "Phil, that's fine, but find something else first before you just up and quit. You know you're a hell of a lot more employable if you're currently working when you apply."

But Phil hadn't been able to endure. His job at a big city post office was just too much! It was driving him crazy. He had often wondered about pursuing an education. He loved learning, and, why not? He could collect unemployment for a while and he was also eligible for the GI Bill.

He remembered that fateful day when he walked into the big boss's office and quit. The guy had tried to talk him out of it, saying what a great job he had been doing and how he had a great future in the organization.

Phil's mind was made up. Nothing would have convinced him. He quit and started on those immediate things he had been thinking about. He applied for unemployment and GI Benefits and got enrolled in a local college, with the intention of studying psychology.

It wasn't long before his next problem confronted him; he found psychology 'so very pedestrian,' but he loved the literature and art classes he was taking. His interest in English literature, and literature in general, led him to form a friendship with one of the English professors and, in spite of his reservations about so quickly dismissing psychology as a vocation and a course of study, he decided to switch to English. For a while he thought he had found his new calling in life, English literature. He thought he would study this to the best of his ability and even go on to an advanced degree.

All this while he was nurturing another pastime, nightlife! It was true, he'd always worked in jobs with hours that kept him out of the night spots most of the time. Phil was absolute in adhering to his work ethic; he never drank on duty, nor had he ever gone to work at all impaired. He was a stickler for sobriety on the job.

So for a brief period while Phil carried on in his new life, studying and evenings out, he sailed along rather smoothly. Occasionally, he would strike up casual relationships with women he would meet on his evenings out, but he never formed any lasting relationships. Similarly, during course work, he had met several young women, but nothing developed there.

As he progressed in his studies, he thought he was doing quite well, but had the rather nebulous feeling that he was treading water, that he now had no clear direction. This feeling was with him a good share of the time, but he carried on in spite of it and pushed such thoughts and feelings aside.

In the spring semester of his junior year, he took a course with an English professor, new to him, and for whom he developed an immediate dislike. This course, *The Bible as Literature*, was a subject near and dear to Phil's heart. All of sudden he found himself in conflict with the professor, who didn't grade his papers with any of the high marks that he had been used to. While up to this point, he had been receiving A's, he now was getting B's and his class participation was not encouraged, as it was in other classes.

Not unlike his experience at the Post Office, Phil was totally unable to maintain his objectivity. Maybe his ego was too tender; he had no idea and didn't care to entertain any other rationales, other than the professor being an asshole! In the aftermath of an unsatisfactory grade on a paper and an equally unpleasant exchange with the professor, he stopped going to class altogether and withdrew from the college.

By this time Phil's unemployment benefits had run out and, of course, his GI educational benefits stopped immediately when he dropped out. With the financial realities impinging on him, he scrounged for work wherever he could find it, working as a carpenter's helper, doing lawn-care, and finding frequent, dirty, odd jobs!

Fortune had not totally abandoned Phil, however, and one day he received a call from one of his former English professors, who told Phil that she had been thinking of him, that he had showed so much promise, and what a tragedy it was that he had dropped out. She urged Phil to come back to college and finish his program. Undoubtedly, this professor was a wise woman, because Phil, being absolutely demoralized in his current life, jumped at the prospect.

Exercising a good deal of effort, with both the college and the Government, Phil managed to get reinstated in his college program and get his GI benefits restored. He did well through his remaining courses. Additionally, to his credit, to satisfy his own sense of standing up to the rigors of the English program, and to satisfy his own self-esteem, he even took another course with the professor that he had clashed with.

Even Phil, who acknowledged few personal accomplishments, was proud of graduating. That his degree was 'With High Honor' was an added satisfaction.

During his years as an undergraduate Phil had several opportunities for apprenticeships in journalism, including one at a local TV station. But he denied any interest in either of these opportunities. Truth be told, he simply couldn't muster the courage. This certainly played into that feeling of treading water, with no clear objective, that he had been nursing throughout his undergraduate years.

Phil continued to indulge his other endeavor, which had become a habit – nightclubbing.

In spite of this uncertainty and lack of clear direction, Phil was admitted to a Ph.D. program in educational psychology almost immediately after graduating.

His feelings surprised him. After the first two weeks in the program he was overwhelmed with foreboding and misgivings. In his mind, he needed a break from studies; it was too intense. Consequently, he withdrew from the graduate program and took a job as a teacher's aide in a junior high school.

Making the choice for the teacher's aide position seemed easy for Phil because he viewed it as a menial job, something beneath him. But again, he was very surprised, as all his former positions were largely in all-male environments and required only marginal social skills.

Now, as a teacher's aide he found himself in a different environment, working mostly with women. It made him anxious and uneasy, even though, objectively, he could see that he was minimally tasked with chores that wouldn't challenge most people.

For Phil, this role put him between a rock and a hard place. Because of this personal challenge he made it a commitment to persevere and stayed throughout the school year. In retrospect, this had been a good experience for him, forcing him to come to grips with a personal dilemma and to succeed.

His experience as a teacher's aide had been very helpful, not only in reducing his social anxiety, but also in exposing him to a field that he chose to pursue.

Phil enrolled in a graduate teaching program the following fall, and ultimately went on to become a freshman English teacher at a local high school. Regarding his dependence on alcohol as a social lubricant, he found as he progressed in his teaching career that he turned ever less frequently to solo nights out and to overindulging. This partly was offset by several relationships and some friendships that he developed in the ensuing years.

WHY, at end of his story: This concludes Phil's story for my purposes, today. Of course, there's much more to his story, but I think as an example of self-actualization, his story offers a good glimpse of some of the issues involved in the maturation process. I'd like to hear comments or I'll take any questions that any of you might have.

REASON: It seems Phil did things for rather obvious reasons, albeit that maybe they weren't very well thought out, but they were Phil's reasons, a result of his perceptions.

WHY: You're generally correct, but really on close inspection one concludes that most of Phil's moves in his life were done in reaction to the circumstances impinging on him. Of course, he had reasons, and, as REASON says, they were very superficial. But I think it should be obvious and an integral part of the story, that eventually, he learned to stop his self-defeating behaviors.

BUT (a late visitor who raises his hand to speak): For all it may seem, this group is ready for a real discussion. I think any solution that you had planned for would be very skewed. I know you all would like to project a direct linear journey from Phil's early, troubled life to one of a settled and productive lifestyle, and to self-actualization. Apparently, you've never thought about the why-nots. Maybe it's not so much the question of why Phil hated his bosses at work, why he fell out with the professor and why he dropped the Ph.D. program or why he drank and chased the nightlife as a social outlet? The question might just as likely be, why not hate those bosses and why not, etc. The way you all are heading, it's like Phil was totally unjustified. I'd be willing to bet that Phil's bosses were really rather poor managers. The professor, well, assuming you've all been undergraduates, I'd like to ask who amongst you has not at one time or another run into a real asshole who's managed some kind of sinecure for himself?

And a Ph.D. program, well, all I can say is you better be ready to have your ass kicked and heart torn out. As for a little nightlife, can you not see the need for Phil's release from the inner turmoil of confronting an ugly, unforgiving world? Maybe Phil was really a genius whose intellect was continually challenged by the ineptitude of bosses, a bombastic professor and a Ph.D. program filled with drudgery! And really, mightn't any one of us have chased the spirits for relief from Phil's world?

WHY: Of course, but this tack is so contrary. What do you think? We're not railroading Phil or something. All you've offered is conjecture. This exercise is to show how Phil triumphed over his personal adversity and overcame personal obstacles and became a usefully whole and functioning adult, self-actualized, even self-possessed, if you will.

BUT, continuing: I say yeah-but, because maturity, what the hell's that anyway? You're supposed to go around kissing others' asses, acting very conventionally, and covering your own ass all the while. Furthermore, what about all those geniuses who bucked convention, unconcerned about social acceptance, and followed their hearts' inspirations, and made so many of the great contributions to civilization? No, of course, they weren't necessarily pleasant ones to be around, but so what? Take Alan Turing for example. The guy was gay. So what? But the social stigma he endured, flying in the face of some tight-ass heterosexuals, while at the same time likely making the world safe for those who couldn't wait to bring him to so-called justice and his ultimate suicide! Or maybe someone like Steve Jobs is more to your liking. Just how personable do you think he was – self-actualized probably, but mature, now that's totally another question. It's also worth considering that some other personality might have handled any of Phil's situations quite differently and have been successful! If you're going to talk self-actualization and maturity, then I sure as hell hope you're thinking of something a lot more than just someone becoming what passes for 'adult' or 'maturity' in this straight-laced rigid world.

ADULT (jumping in): Now wait just a minute! You come in here, uninvited I might add, and start throwing around a lot of invective and insinuations. On some level, you may have a point, in that most beings don't have what it takes to be a Jobs or Turing. In fact, most of mankind, including us, just muddle through life. Besides, if you want to get along you have to rub elbows at some level. Maybe maturity is learning how to get along, so you can travel through adulthood without trampling over everyone.

REASON: Yeah, I think it's recognizing that you can't have everything in life, so you learn what's important to you, and then you spend your life striving for that, and you complete your sense of self, satisfy your ego, so to speak. I think being mature is a continual state of mind, where one is comfortable in his or her own skin. You come to know who you are and can afford to give a little elbow room to others, as they come down the pike, maybe even give others a leg up, when you perceive it would be valuable to do so. I don't think being a genius is any measure of determining maturity.

HOW: Just *how* does this all square with the world as we know it? Generally speaking one is considered mature when they are self-assured and are able to make room for others and comport themselves with a good deal of self-restraint.

WHEN: You have to wonder, though, just *when* one knows they've arrived? You know, just when are you mature – eighteen, twenty-one, forty, or when?

WHERE: It's certainly worth asking, is anyone mature all the time, any place, any-*where*? I've noticed that often one may appear mature in one place and be totally out of sorts in another. Or to put it another way, in most circumstances one may act totally composed and comport himself with a high degree of self-confidence, but then some circumstance will come along and they just totally lose it.

WHO: Yes, *who* amongst us is perfect? Oh, some may lead exemplary lives, but that doesn't mean they don't ever screw up.

WHAT: *What* is life all about? To me life is spontaneity; anything less is just existence. So, one comports oneself with some degree of control mostly, but expression being the very nature of personality, there are those times when personalities are bound to clash. Is one not mature if they get into a fight with someone else? So, you lose it for a moment, that shouldn't be the defining moment of your life.

WHY: *Why* not call a spade a spade? I ask myself, is it not inherent in human nature, and subsequently the way we as words comport ourselves, that behavior is a fickle, transient thing. Man is a social animal and certain norms and conventions of social decorum have developed as a means of allowing society to function. Maybe the answer to questions of how, when, where, who, what and why, *maturity*, is that it's just a social norm, something like a moving target? Maturity is a state of being, one moment you have it and the next moment you may lose it. Of course, some appear to be able to sustain long periods of maturity, before they go off the reservation and lose it momentarily because of some silly behavior.

BUT: Maybe not. There are those models of decorum…

ADULT, interrupting and talking over BUT: No buts about it. For the purposes of our discussion the questions carry the day, especially when considered in the light of reason. I'd like to ask my understudy what he thinks.

KYLE: Growing up is tough! It's easy for all of you, sitting back and coming up with all these ideas. Let me tell you when you're in the middle of it, I say maturity, who the hell really knows or cares, for that matter? I remember when I was trying to put the plug in the jug, so to speak. You want to talk self-actualization, let me tell you, you learn pretty fast that you have to start taking responsibility for your own life, if you want to stay sober. But you also come to know that you can't do it alone; money won't do it, material things won't do it and fancy titles won't get you anywhere either. You learn you have to join the human race and make some real friends. Another little tidbit, you have to accept you're not the center of the universe and the only thing you need to know about God is you're not him/her. You learn pretty fast to keep centered in the day, trying to live one day at a time. So I like to think I grew up the hard way—mature, I don't know, but I finally got my act together and I show up for life every day, whatever it may bring. Although, God knows, I never expected this.

However, if I was giving advice, I'd say try to figure out what it is you want to do in life and then go after it. In my mind, you learn pretty fast you won't get too far by stepping on the wrong toes. So yeah, someone said it earlier, you kiss a few asses and try to get by. Oh, yeah, you also get up in a few faces too, but so far in life all I see is a muddle, more like survival, especially in this place.

Now I find myself an adult, chronologically at least, stuck in places not by choice, but I'm trying to make do until I learn how to get out, if that's even possible?

BUT (speaking to ADULT): If I may say, after all this harangue, it appears Kyle has said it best, so the real question is just who is tutoring whom?

Curtains come down

There was resounding applause as MUSIC stepped back to the podium. "Thank you, thank you," he said, and continuing, "Are there any comments or questions from the audience?"

THESPIAN, sitting next to Kyle, stood and asked, "Is this play supposed to be a new form of drama?"

"What do you mean," MUSIC asked.

"Well, it looks very predatory to me. I mean you get a total novice up on the stage and put him in a part where all he can do is react, since he doesn't really know the script or what the outcome is supposed to be," THESPIAN said.

"Well, recognizing that our visitor may not have known the full implications of what psychodrama is, I guess you could say it was a bit of an initiation – a new learning experience. Is that so bad?" MUSIC said.

Kyle, who had taken his seat back in the audience by then, jumped up from his chair yelling, "I think it was very unfair to spring such a trap on me or anyone!"

"Seems to me you fell right into the part and did an excellent job," MUSIC said.

"I guess you think flattery will get you everywhere. As far as I can see, any idiot could have played my part. It was really just 'playing the fool,' and I sure as hell felt like a dunce," Kyle said.

"I understand, and I'm sorry that you feel you were duped, but I hope you learned the valuable lesson that you can carry off most anything, if you just accept the role you've been handed. There you were and you played your part to a tee, or to quote the great bard Shakespeare, *All's Well That Ends Well*! Not to diminish, of course, the essence of the play you were just in, demonstrating the value of the question on the road to maturity, most notably *'Why?'* I hope you at least learned that," MUSIC said.

"Oh, yes! I've learned a lot more than *'Why?'* Things like cover your ass and expecting the unexpected come to mind!"

"Now really, you know 'life is an education' and you seem to be getting on quite well, as far as I can see," MUSIC asserted.

MUSIC called on another word. It was SONG, who was sitting next to G-CLEF, "I think it's time for a little music to lighten the mood," she said. After all, our visitor has endured his initiation very well and G-CLEF, myself and some others, certainly want to welcome him and show him the lighter side of life. Our little performance is called:

SONG OF MUSIC

Where'er the strains of music go, so lifted are the hearts of all. From chorus, symphony, and opera, the timbered notes do call.

Souls and minds are soothed or stirred at their vital cores, while notes of music fill the air, lifting hearts to lighten worldly chores.

Music of the spheres, music to the ears, music, music, music.

Where sorrow or sadness reign, spirits are lifted and hearts are soothed,
by strains of music-filling-air, for life's burdens so removed.

No heart too hard, nor sorrow too deep, for music's joyous essence,
to touch the very core of souls, who offer up their presence.

Music for the tears, music for the years, music, music, music.

With strangers in our midst, we take them in our hearts to hold.
In the Eternal's bosom, there's room for all, life's praises to be told.

Imagine our world a haven, souls living peacefully together, celebrating differences, finding all more alike than ever.

Music for freedom from fears, music for heartfelt cheers, music, music, music."

As SONG was going on, Kyle got up and walked back out into the other hall and then exited that hall where he had entered the *Painting, Drawing and Sculpting Conference.*

"Well, that's the last of that. Jesus, that was enough to curl anyone's hair. A play, of all things, about self-actualization. Alright, already, I am an adult and I sure would love to put all this bullshit behind me and just let go and get on with life, if that's even possible," Kyle said to himself, as he pushed the exit button on the handles in the virtual reality console, also remembering, this time, to remove the helmet. Sure enough, there he was, just sitting in front of the computer. He reached over to the keyboard and touched the *enter* button and when he did so, to his utter surprise, this odd thing that looked something like an oversized peanut was sitting there! Just then it opened up and it was the 'Eye' who had been resting and had his lid down.

"What is it now? Can't you see that I'm trying to catch a few rays and a little shuteye? It's my day off you know and I was sunbathing."

"How can it be your day off, it's Tuesday?" Kyle asked.

"I take every seventh day off, but what's it to you anyway?"

"Oh, nothing," Kyle said, "but now that you say so, it seems odd that the seventh day ends on a Tuesday."

"It's the seventh day from whenever I want it to be."

"So, you'll be in tomorrow?"

"Maybe or maybe not. I may decide to take tomorrow off too. Let's see, that's seven days from last Wednesday, I think," the Eye mused.

"That's crazy. You might as well just say you take any day off you want and leave it at that."

"Haven't you got enough problems of your own? You come along here, wake me, disturb my sunbathing and just make a general pest of yourself. What are you doing here anyway? I thought you were off to study Remedial Grammar or some such truck."

"It's a long story and I'm supposed to be looking for that now, but to be honest I'm not very excited about the prospects. God, I feel so stuck here in these strange worlds of letters and words. Is there any way that you can help me get out of here?"

"I see you're still having trouble accepting your lot in life, and you're still looking for others to solve your problems."

"Everyone in this place just expects me to follow along. Is this your idea of being self-possessed?" Kyle fumed.

"Look sonny, patience is the name of the game in life. You want everything yesterday. Give it time and apply yourself to what's in front of you."

"I have to admit, you're probably right, but I'm thinking of the here and now. I sure want to get back to my former world."

"Well, I know those two who were helping you meant well, so I'll get you headed in that direction if you like. You should catch up with them there. Just put your helmet back on and I'll direct you."

"You better not be screwing around with me," Kyle retorted.

"Wouldn't dream of it!" the Eye chuckled.

REMEDIAL GRAMMAR

The second Kyle put his helmet on he was immersed in a large open area. To his surprise there were WORD and THOUGHT.

"What a strange place; it reminds me of my days in the army!" Kyle said, then muttering, "It looks something like a parade ground; God, how I hated those affairs!"

Indeed, it did look something like a parade ground. It appeared as a large open field with all kinds of strange objects running around. And while it was hard to tell what was happening, Kyle knew there was some master plan to it.

Turning to WORD, Kyle exclaimed, "What's going on? I thought this was supposed to be English Grammar. All I see are these strange words running around and I can't make heads or tails of anything!"

"Oh, yes, this is where it all begins and ends," WORD started to explain. "It's here that words get together to give meaning to their lives and to get on with their purpose of being."

"What the hell are you talking about?" Kyle protested.

"Stop right there!" WORD interjected. "Surely you've heard of the Sentence, the Paragraph, the Chapter, etc.? Well, our comrades are just getting arranged into coherent segments that are readily understood and that often add to larger statements, concepts and compositions that then end up as conversations, articles, books and the like."

Just as WORD was explaining this, an object that looked just like a majorette with the word MARSHAL on his chest approached Kyle and his two companions. "You three! Assume your positions. What are you doing standing around?"

"We're just observing," THOUGHT replied.

"Well, get out of the way and go to the Reviewing Stand if you're observing or 'in-waiting!' the MARSHAL commanded.

"In-waiting, what the hell's he talking about?" Kyle asked.

"Oh that's when you're waiting for your turn to join a group of other letters and words to form a sentence, etc."

"Well, I'm certainly not ready for that," Kyle replied.

"I agree," both his companions chimed in at once.

"They're having grammar lessons out back right now, and I think we better get you there ASAP!" WORD said, adding, "Before you have a conniption!"

THOUGHT and WORD guided Kyle to a structure, bordering the field, where they went inside to an area that seemed to be in absolute bedlam.

"And this is supposed to be where they teach grammar!" Kyle cried out.

"You'll see," THOUGHT replied.

Just then a word was protesting to another word, "But I don't want to be a noun. I want to be a verb."

"You can't be a verb, you're a noun, and that's it!" said the word that looked like a teacher's ferule, and who was obviously the instructor.

"What d' yeah mean, I can't! I don't want to be treated as just a dumb ANKLE! I want some action too!" said the word, that looked something like a pipe-fitting.

"Oh, and how's that supposed to sound or fit in with other words?" the instructor asked.

"Easy," ANKLE replied. "So maybe somebody just wants to 'ankle' over to see their uncle Wally or maybe they want to ankle down to see the foot doctor, if you'll pardon the pun. It's that simple, you see."

"Oh, so you think you're a verb now or you want to become a verb. You do know there's a word for your kind? But you're not going to become a gerund or a verbal-noun; it's not going to happen on my watch!" the Instructor said.

"My father told me that English was flexible," ANKLE protested.

"Look, sonny, it doesn't happen just like that. It has to come into common discourse and usage before you just jump in, especially in the written word," the instructor said.

"But how's it ever going to happen if someone doesn't just start using it?" the puzzled ANKLE asked.

"Just a minute, I'll address this later."

"How timely," the instructor said to a visitor who just entered the room. "Class," he continued, "I want to introduce our visitor ETYMOLOGY."

ETYMOLOGY, who Kyle had met earlier, still looked the same, with a picture of WORD, on her cover, and when she shifted her position, even slightly, the emoji changed its appearance. Kyle, still confused about her appearance, asked WORD what was going on.

WORD said, "Oh, she just shows me in my many iterations. You do know I've been around for a while and she is just trying to capture my essence – not the easiest job in the world, I'll grant you, but if anyone can do it..."

The Instructor was going on, "Now, class, this is an excellent time to address the confusion brought up by your classmate and the noun ANKLE. He says he wants to act as a verb, but most of you know if you're a noun, you're a noun – not a verb." Then turning to ETYMOLOGY, he continued, "I hope our esteemed visitor, whose entire existence has been devoted to the history of words and their usage, can explain this to all of you, not least to ANKLE, of course."

"Well, that's a rather simple explanation of nouns and verbs," ETYMOLOGY said. Turning to ANKLE, she continued, "In your case, of course, that may be the best way to look at it. You don't deny you're a noun, do you? But, even though right now there's no reason for you to act out and become a verb; that doesn't mean it won't ever happen. As recently as 1892 your relative KNEE came-out and started acting like a verb, so don't lose hope." Then chuckling, she went on, "Of course, it's really not very nice to knee someone, do yeah think? Now in your case, you do have a history that you can be proud of. Yes, you're descended from Old English with probably some Old Norse and Old Frisian, including other influences. That certainly establishes you as a word of some significance and standing, if you'll pardon the pun. This is not to say that there aren't many words that act as both nouns and verbs, and I don't want to confuse you, but in your case, it seems likely that you'll remain a noun, that is, until you're included in the local vernacular as a verb, as you've already suggested, or, otherwise, until some notable pundit starts seeing and saying things your way. But it's certainly not up to you to initiate the transition. It's also important to know that the language can't change too fast. Otherwise it might become unintelligible like the situation that developed at the *Tower*... We're still trying to recover from that fiasco."

"Now, I know this is confusing to everyone, so I came here today with a little story that I think should add some clarity to our roles in life. It's about <u>Doubt</u>, <u>Acceptance</u> and <u>Change</u>, things we all experience at one time or another and in themselves raise issues of ambiguity. They are addressed in another manner by the ancient bard, Shakespeare, who asked, 'What's in a name? That which we call a rose, by any other name would smell as sweet.'"

"Also, it's a story about the life of one of our visitors today, Mr. Kyle Wilson. Kyle please stand and take a bow."

Amidst the clapping, Kyle, dumbfounded, rose from his seat, saying to himself, "here we go again, another roasting."

ETYMOLOGY went on, "Thank you all and thank you Kyle for coming to my little performance here today. I call this story:

TO BE

Even though Kyle came from a loving family and was a wanted child, the only way to adequately describe his childhood family was dysfunctional! It was an extended family, including his mother, two aunts and his grand-parents. His grandfather was a bit of a curmudgeon and family control was largely matriarchal in nature. His earlier family life, with just his mother, father and two siblings was disrupted at the age of four when his mother had a nervous breakdown. This episode was very traumatic for Kyle. He, an older sister and brother moved in with his grandparents and two aunts in Nashua, New Hampshire. His father remained behind to continue his position as a herdsman in a nearby state, visiting the family on weekends. After a long hospital stay, his mother came to the home in Nashua, which became the family's permanent home. Several years after moving to Nashua a younger sister was born.

With exposure to alcohol, proffered by a favorite uncle in his early teens, drinking became a frequent escape from the inner turmoil and confusion he experienced in those early years. His drinking increased during his teen and high school years, although he was also quite engaged in life and had held several different jobs by the time he graduated.

During his high school years, he didn't participate in any extracurricular activities, nor was he a particularly good student. He was, more or less, a class clown, interjecting teenage humor and disrupting the class to get attention, though never maliciously. His school years were largely filled with fanciful thinking and daydreaming. His mother had read extensively to Kyle and his siblings when they were younger, so he was really quite precocious. His teachers liked him and many thought he had great potential, but they also found him difficult to help develop and mature. When he finally did graduate, it was with no academic accomplishments, no scholastic direction and not even a trade or specific skill to take him into life. At that point his means of self-sufficiency was a full-time position as a factory worker in a local plastics company.

This background was really a strange admixture for a young man who was by nature very curious and natively intelligent. He was a keen observer and generally a quick study, especially of anything to do with mechanics. On the other hand, he was not at all able to promote himself and he lived with an abiding fear of failure.

These conflicting elements in his early life led him to become easily bored, and he was hungering for excitement and change. To meet this need he decided to join the U.S. Military. A good friend from high school had joined shortly after graduating. After repeated efforts by a local Air Force recruiter and in spite of his doubt about his abilities, his fear of the unknown and his lack of self-confidence, he also felt compelled to join and ultimately made the decision to do so, even though he was terrified.

Not having had a male role model in his formative years very likely played a large part in Kyle's very difficult adjustment to military indoctrination. At any rate, he was not used to being yelled at! Such niceties as "please, thank you, may I," were certainly not part of his new military world. Nor were the sergeants at all interested in what he thought, or how he was feeling. One example that was to stick in his memory throughout his life happened on the first day of his arrival at boot camp. After being assembled into a squadron and listening to the first dos and don'ts of military life, the group was told to enter the barracks and pick a bunk. Everyone was to first remove their shoes before entering. So Kyle, like his comrades, dutifully removed his shoes, but unlike everyone else, he left his shoes on the stoop immediately outside the doorway, having heard that this is what people did in many other parts of the world. As was the custom back then, the sergeant, waiting for someone to use as an example to demonstrate his authority through total humiliation, immediately called Kyle out in front of the entire group. He deftly flung his shoes far across an open area and under another billet nearby, making Kyle chase after them and crawl under that building to retrieve them while yelling and mocking him. Kyle was totally unprepared for these crude treatments and the military's indifference to personal feelings. In spite of this, he managed to adjust and finally to graduate from basic training, though not without several other equally humiliating experiences.

He often cursed himself for his decision to join, but he also saw his commitment as something he could not turn his back on no matter how humiliating; his pride was totally at stake and, equally important, he saw himself as irrevocably trapped without any recourse.

From boot camp, he was sent to a specialized Air Force school for training in communications. He did well at the school and got along very well with his fellow recruits, although he was lonely. In spite of having a couple of very good friends, he drank quite frequently. At these times, he would be quite assertive, ebullient and, very often, the life of the party. One time while at this school he met a young woman who was quite appealing and they struck it off enough for Kyle to ask her to join him that evening. They met and he took her to dinner at the Base Exchange and they then walked around the base. As they walked he wondered about kissing her and what would come after, but he was terrified of being rejected. At the end of the evening he was able only to kiss her goodnight and he walked away feeling very empty. He was totally confused. He had been a gentleman, but is that what it means to be a gentleman and why was he afraid to make a move, what was wrong? He didn't have a clue, only that he felt totally out of place!

The military, on balance, was a very difficult life for Kyle. After graduation, he was given a rather choice assignment to an airbase in Japan. He lived in fear most of the time and in this foreign land, where most airmen seemed to be happy, he felt lonely. At this point, like so many of his fellows, he turned more and more to alcohol.

Although one of his friends hooked him up with a very nice woman in the town outside the base, she meant little to him, as by this time his off-duty hours were largely spent carousing with friends and chasing the bar scene outside the airbase. It wasn't long before this woman, who really liked him, also realized that he was incorrigible and stopped seeing him. Kyle was not at all dismayed by her dropping him and he didn't take it personally because he knew, objectively, she was justified.

Occasionally he would hook up with other women he met while on the town, but he really was totally self-absorbed, spent most of his off-duty time drinking and when he ran out of money, a regular situation between paydays, he could usually be found at the base library.

He had, after all, been a precocious child and introspection was a large part of his inner life. Romance, other than the physical act of sex, was beyond his social skills and probably due to his early childhood trauma he would not let anyone, either man or woman, get too close.

His fear of rejection outweighed his need for genuine acceptance and love. Drinking and intellectual introspection offered him the only solace and solution to his life. He was, after all, as the song goes, looking for love and acceptance in all the wrong places! Unfortunately, he continued on a path that led him to such a lonely and desperate place that he finally attempted suicide and was mustered out of the military with an honorable discharge for medical reasons.

Kyle had become an unwitting victim of his own dysfunctional personality. After his discharge, he took several different jobs, continued drinking off hours, and, while drunk, made a couple of unsuccessful suicide attempts. Ultimately, in a stressful period, he made a very serious suicide attempt and was discovered just in time. This led to hospitalization at a Veterans Hospital, where he received extensive therapy, including vocational counseling and an educational rehab program that included college, where he studied English with a minor in journalism.

College and the study of English literature were a great diversion for a young man with his native intellectual abilities and his psychological issues. Kyle was an 'A' student, graduating cum laude, but he hadn't changed at all regarding his fear of rejection and social situations. He had, however, managed to cultivate pseudo sociability that served him quite well in pursuing his studies and all related social functions.

In spite of all his psychotherapy, he continued to drink, but he did make attempts to control his drinking and to some degree he was successful for a number of years.

It was during these college years that he rekindled his love of literature that his mother had nurtured in his childhood and that he had furtively fed throughout his turbulent earlier years. In his daydreams, he often envisioned writing the great American novel, but whenever he tried it was never quite right. It seemed to Kyle that in reality writing was a very torturous process. He wrote several short pieces and a few poems that the family thought were very cute, but those things never went any further than that. In Kyle's mind, they weren't real writing, at least in any professional sense.

During college, with his minor in journalism, he wrote one feature article for the school newspaper that was quite a success and he also did an internship at a radio station, where he was actually preparing news feeds and writing short pieces for broadcast. He did not like the pressure of deadlines and the superficial nature of radio news, a rationale for not pursuing broadcast news. When he was offered a job by a local TV station, he turned it down saying that type of reporting was superficial, and that he wanted to focus more on news stories for print journalism.

In this same time period, he wrote a short story, *Another Pimple for Bobbie*, a story about a young man struggling for identity and initiation into adulthood. He sent it to a magazine: although, he didn't get an outright rejection, he got a letter from an editor suggesting changes and what the editor would like to see, of anything he wanted to send for submission. Kyle was indifferent to this response. In his eyes, the editor had validated his ability to write, but Kyle wouldn't pander, and besides this story was really a lightweight piece in his mind, rather trivial, and so never responded. Kyle's mind went instead to the grandiose, the great novel, something that would gain the attention and acclaim he craved!

After college, Kyle wanted to see if he really could write a bona fide short story and so he wrote another short piece, *The Curse of Douglas Fairchild Roth*, a story about a young man in the early stages of alcoholism, trying to understand his world, not knowing he was addicted. The story took an ironic twist, ending with this protagonist discovering that his future was most likely that of an alcoholic! This story went nowhere. Kyle didn't even try to get it published, but in a strange way he was satisfied he could do it, but again he saw it as a rather trivial narrative and not worth pursuing!

After getting his bachelor's degree, Kyle held several good jobs. One job he really liked was as a library technician in a Government library. Though he was still drinking at this time, his interest in library work spurred him on to pursue a Master's Degree in Library and Information Science.

It was during the pursuit of this degree while working full-time that he realized drinking was seriously interfering with his life, but he also quickly learned he was unable to stop drinking on his own. Fortunately, he found a 12-step program that worked. He sobered up in time to graduate. Degree in hand, he left his job as a library technician to take a position as a credited librarian at the university where he is currently employed as a supervisor.

Sobriety brought Kyle many gifts, and, in this position, he does a lot of commercial writing as well as managing ongoing projects. This has taught Kyle the great lesson of what it takes to write a substantial document. He learned to deal with his fear of failure, of not being able to write something that was good enough. He realized that writing was an awful lot about discipline, putting oneself in a chair and just doing it. Of course, he also realized that this type of writing was somewhat perfunctory, at least in the sense that his own ego and self-esteem weren't completely at stake.

One day while window shopping, he met a young saleswoman, Priscilla, in a music store at the mall. She was tall and thin with fine features and long brown hair. But there was a sadness and preoccupation that Kyle saw behind her beautiful face. She was absolutely without affect. Kyle found she was very gentle to talk with and very gifted at the piano, despite a deep sense of detachment and melancholy when she spoke.

After talking for a few moments, Kyle asked her why she was just selling pianos and not playing professionally. She told Kyle a tragic story about her life and how she ended up selling pianos. Her father, a celebrity, a piano virtuoso, had forbidden that she become a public performer.

Kyle was completely taken by the saleswoman's story! For the rest of that day it consumed him and during the next days he found himself reflecting on her tragic life. Another weekend found him at the same mall looking for her, but sadly she was not there. By this time, he realized he could not get her out of his mind. He was sure that some caprice of fate or even the muses had spoken directly to him! This was great tragedy; this was the making of a really great story! All these years he had been dreaming about writing and thinking of the great stories he would write, and right here this unbelievable life story had dropped into his lap!

As Kyle mulled over the sales-woman's tragic life, it consumed him and strangely he felt a kinship to her. He decided he would write her story come 'hell or high water'! He titled his story, *Cognitive Dissonance*, a story he became proud of as much for the act of completing it and trusting his own voice for its artistic dimensions. Finally, he felt in his gut that he now could write without paralyzing fear! This fear certainly had hindered him in the past, but by this point in his life he realized why this had been so painful. It had been the fear of failure because his work in his idealized world had to be perfect, and that is an ideal setup for failure.

At this point in Kyle's life, he had an unfortunate turn of events and became the victim of a serious auto accident, suffering a serious head injury and subsequently ending up in a coma and was later determined to be nearly braindead. Even though his prognosis remains uncertain, he has made quite a bit of progress in adjusting and modifying his world view and his perspective on life since that time. We certainly want him to know as well that he is welcomed here as long he wishes to stay with us.

This, my friends, concludes my story about Kyle, but we hold out hope for new chapters in his life and also that new chapters in his creative world will be written, but that, of course, we cannot know at this point.

ETYMOLOGY had ended her story, but then, while the class gave no clear evidence that they knew it had ended, she said, "So what do I have to do, spell it out for you? Doubt and acceptance, does anyone not see the connection here? And you, ANKLE, can you accept your role as a noun and isn't your hope to become a verb a rather dubious endeavor?"

ETYMOLOGY went on, "This would be a good time for any questions or comments regarding Kyle's transformation or any other aspect of this story that touches on doubt, acceptance and change."

Suddenly an undercurrent of conversation became apparent as two words in the back of the room started talking loudly to each other. PSYCHOLOGY and PSYCHIATRY had raised their voices in what was obviously a heated discussion, and suddenly they could be heard by everyone!

"You'll never understand what an important part doubt plays in shaping a person's personality and future," said PSYCHOLOGY, who looked just like the capitol Greek letter Psi.

"It's accepting one's heritage and social environment! It's self-acceptance, you idiot!" said PSYCHIATRY, who looked like the letter Psi, but with a caduceus imposed on the center of it.

"Stop it, you two!" ETYMOLOGY interjected. "This is a civilized class and I do expect a certain amount of decorum!

You both will get your chance to help settle this issue in good time."

"Now, does anyone in the class want to summarize the story or tell us what the dynamics of it are?"

Raising his hand, VERISIMILITUDE, who looked like TRUTH, but a smaller torch and casting a white light over all his surroundings, was called upon to speak. "Doubt is that bogeyman that hounds most mortals who have a conscience, but who also feel compelled to speak and act in spite of their fear. They are both the small and large voices that move society, hopefully in positive directions. And those with little or no doubt, like the Hitlers of this world, sadly tear apart and undo the good in the world. Doubt is indeed the instigator of self-examination that speaks to our better angels and moves the more fortunate mortals amongst us to a higher moral plane."

"Rubbish and poppycock!" yelled PSYCHIATRY. "What are you doing here anyway? I thought TRUTH was supposed to be attending this class and since when do you speak for him?"

"Yes, normally TRUTH would be addressing these types of situations, but he was called away to a significant trial in town, where JUSTICE was on trial for his life, and he needs a rest. Of course, anything I say will be 'very similar' to what TRUTH would say."

"Enough, already!" ETYMOLOGY cried. "Okay, PSYCHIATRY, let's hear your thoughts on the issue."

"Well, it was obviously Kyle's gradual acceptance of himself, warts and all – so to speak – that helped him gain mastery over his life. His self-acceptance was the vehicle that allowed him to grow and change. As he tried new things, his level of self-assurance grew and he was able to make the succeeding changes that ultimately led him to be fully comfortable in his own skin," PSYCHIATRY said.

"What about that?" ETYMOLOGY said to PSY-CHOLOGY. "What's your full take on Kyle's development?"

"PSYCHIATRY'S points are well taken, but we can never diminish the role of doubt. After all, doubt is the engine of self-reflection and this was the force that prompted Kyle to weigh the factors, rational and irrational, that impinged on him and that finally allowed him to break free of the fear of ego annihilation and to ultimately become a free agent acting in his own best interest," PSYCHOLOGY replied.

VERISIMILITUDE had his hand up again and was next to speak. "While both points are well taken and would appear to represent the situation as it unfolded in the story, I would like to also point out Kyle's efforts in seeking out a 12-step program and his willingness to confront his addiction to alcohol. Surely attending such a program not only shows his self-doubt of his ability to handle this alone, but also, the beginnings of his acceptance of himself as flawed and demonstrates a willingness to reach outside himself for help."

"Let's not forget that not everyone is going to become a Voltaire or an Abe Lincoln. Most folks just muddle through, exercising a good deal of deceit and ignorance before they shed their mortal coil! A trail of debris usually follows in the wake of most mortals, with but a few achievements to hang their reputations on," PSYCHIATRY said.

"Can I speak?" MANIFESTATION yelled, while raising his hand. "Isn't this all just Monday-morning quarter-backing? These two shrinks can make a case for anything. What if Kyle turned into an axe-murderer; what would they say then? 'Oh, he just didn't know his place in the world and, filled with doubt of his own reality, he acted on impulses that someone, well adjusted, would quickly dismiss out of hand! They would just say, in essence, that he accepted himself with an antisocial manifestation. So, I say yes, to answer the ancient bard's question (*what's in a name?*), doubt, acceptance – it's all the same; it's really just a way of describing a personal viewpoint, but neither is the be-all and end-all in describing Kyle's journey to a successful midlife. A thousand other descriptions would do just as well. Why not just say he gradually became well adjusted, after dealing with both internal and external forces that hindered his development?"

ANKLE jumped from his seat saying, "For all this talk, I don't see any consensus. What's in a name, I'll tell you, nothing! That's right, nothing. You guys have turned doubt and acceptance into meaningless terms. How am I to apply this in my situation? Don't tell me. I know, I know! Just suck it up, like everything else in this world. Things happen when the undefined powers-that-be say so and not before, and I have little or no say in it. What am I to think; a noun's a noun, until someone else decides it can be a verb and I'm just supposed to sit back and suck it up? All this palaver from ETYMOLOGY and the rest of you and I don't have a clue. What's more, if someone ever does decide to ankle somewhere or other, then I'm very likely to become lost in the shuffle and I won't know who the hell I am anymore!"

At this WORD stood up to speak, "ANKLE has a point you know. Why, just a year or so ago the Oxford Dictionaries named an emoji, the pictograph – not the word, as its Word-of-the-Year, and then, later and to my utter surprise, Kyle Wilson accused me of looking like an emoji, so now I'm reduced to a pictograph on someone else's whim! What a world!"

At this, ETYMOLOGY recognized INTENTIONALITY, who had his hand up.

"Just a few words, if I may, whoever said words were perfect. A more nuanced understanding may be the very reason why ANKLE someday may actually function as a verb. There's so much more to language when we are caught up in discussion or in the written word. For spoken words, there is inflection, body language, the mood of the moment and the overall context of the conversation. For the written word, thoughts and ideas are usually more carefully arranged and this arrangement, coupled with context and mood, are what convey meaning and intention. Sadly, over and above all this, of course, in both speaking and writing, confusion and miscommunication do still take place. So, what's in a name, quite often, intention is of the particular moment. When a word is spoken or when it's written, it may have its meaning diminished, enhanced or changed in some subtle way by the larger context. Our friend WORD, who once adorned clay tablets or rolled off of tongues for eons, but who now, in the contemporary world, finds that his additional form of expression is an emoji! Need I say more!"

After all this, Kyle was raising his hand and squirming in his chair.

ETYMOLOGY finally acknowledged him. "And now, my fellow words, I defer to Kyle, a visitor from another world, and I hasten to add, on the matter at hand, his will be the last word!"

Kyle started, "My friends and other words, if I've learned anything here in the Land of Letters, the Land of Words and all its adjoining realms, it is that nothing is certain, nothing is forever, and everything is up for grabs, especially in this place. But change – well, that takes place everywhere and in everything. People change, words change; albeit mostly for the better, but sadly, sometimes for the worst. I was bound to change, in spite of myself. However the world impinges on us, we all change. After all, who would want to remain the same forever, as just a stick in the mud, so to speak? Please don't take offense, but regarding the recent exposition by ETYMOLOGY and others, I've never heard so much gobbledygook in all my life. For me, when I want to say something, I speak my piece and say what's on my mind. I just assume that those I'm talking to understand what I'm saying; if not they'll inquire further. If I'm writing and I'm uncertain of a particular word, then I refer to the dictionary. All in all, I say let the chips fall where they may. I don't need to stand every sentence on its head just to make an utterance, nor do I have to parse every phrase that comes my way. As for you, ANKLE, I say learn to go with the flow. When the time comes for you to act as a verb, worry about that then; in the meantime, enjoy your role in the world, find another pair of ankles to get-it-on with and just immerse yourself in life."

"I think this pretty much covers it for our friend," WORD said. "Come on, Kyle," and the three of them strode off.

HOMEWARD BOUND

Kyle felt something wet on his face and then heard, "Kyle, dear, how are you, are you in there, sweetheart?" and then tearfully, "Really, Doctor Swanson, how much longer can this go on?"

Kyle knew it was her.

"Betsy!" He tried yelling, but nothing came out.

"Well, it's really hard to tell. I have to tell you, here at Pine View, it's not uncommon for these things to drag out for months and, unfortunately, there are those who never wake up," Doctor Swanson replied.

"My dear Kyle, whatever is going to become of him? I can't bear it," Betsy cried.

"Please, Ms. Flemming, go home and try to get some rest. We'll notify you if there's any change."

Suddenly, Betsy noticed tears running down Kyle's cheeks. "Doctor," she screamed pointing to Kyle's face, "he's crying."

"Oh, my God, those are real tears, brought on by your visit, not just an autonomic response," Dr. Swanson said.

"For Christ's sake, they finally brought me to tears," Kyle said to himself. "Jesus, at last I finally got someone's attention and now they know somebody's home."

"Don't worry, Ms. Flemming, this is a good sign. I'll call Dr. Angle, and they'll likely be transporting him back to Methuen General."

"Kyle, pay attention! Where's your head at? We've got places to go and things to do," WORD cried.

The strange voices were fading as Kyle mumbled, "Yeah, sure, God, will I ever get out of here?"

By now somewhat used to being torn between two worlds, Kyle paid little attention as he was shuttled back to Methuen Hospital.

"Well, let's get going. We're supposed to go up to the set for a little exercise before the main event," WORD said.

"What event? What have you guys got up to now?" Kyle demanded.

"Oh, it's nothing really. Just the rehearsal before the main event up at the place you call the Parade Ground, where we were some time ago," WORD replied.

"Oh, God," Kyle moaned.

The building they went to wasn't very far from the area they had just come from.

"Here we are," said THOUGHT.

Kyle looked up and could see a sign over the front entrance, *The Theatre of the Absurd and Where Stories Come to Life.* "Oh my God, what the hell am I in for now," he sighed.

As they walked in, SENTENCE, a quill pen, came up to them. "Is this the one you were telling me about?" SENTENCE said to WORD.

"The very same," WORD replied.

"I see what you were saying," SENTENCE said.

"What the hell are you two doing? Never mind talking about me, if that isn't bad enough, introductions might be nice and just maybe you'd include me in whatever's going on!" Kyle yelled.

"So sorry!" WORD apologized. "This is SENTENCE and he's been kind enough to come by for a little instructional performance for you to get your feet wet."

"Get my feet wet? What are you guys planning now? You folks sure have a different way of welcoming folks."

"Be quiet!" THOUGHT said. "Just listen for a minute before you go off, will you?"

"Hi Kyle," SENTENCE said. "I've planned a little rehearsal, so you'll be prepared for your maiden journey when the time comes."

"And just what journey are you talking about?" Kyle asked angrily.

"Well, you're not planning on staying here forever, are you?"

"God, no! I sure as hell hope not," Kyle replied.

"Well, don't be alarmed. This is nothing really. It's just another form of socialization, something I think you'll get the drift of very quickly. You know, it's fine to hang out with WORD and THOUGHT and other words, but we all have a place in the world you know, and it's time you got on with the business of getting involved in the discourse of this world. After all, you're certainly more than just a casual visitor."

"What are you talking about? I didn't have any choice getting here. You should know, nearly braindead, coma, car accident and all that juicy stuff. At least you should know it, everyone else seems to know my entire life's story."

"Oh, come on, do you think any of us had a choice getting into this world? Sure, some things we do have a say about, but really, we start out on a blank slate and fate surely plays a part in all our lives!" SENTENCE said. "Anyway, we're not here to debate determinism, so let's get on with the show."

Then SENTENCE went on to introduce many of his colleagues. "Kyle, I'd like to introduce you to today's stage managers, SUBJECT, PREDICATE, PARAGRAPH and COMPOSITION. Now you might think you're back at the beginning of your journey here as you look over our cast of characters, but I think you'll quickly appreciate how well they play together. My colleagues have been doing this for some time and have really followed their script very well, so we're going to open with just a small part of the first act to give you an idea of how things work here…"

Kyle could hear the opening strains of Hayden's *Surprise Symphony* as the curtains opened and letters started streaming across the stage in various groups. At first he couldn't quite get the drift of what was going on, but all of a sudden it became completely obvious as more and more letters strode forth onto the stage.

"My, he certainly is odd looking."

"I wonder what he is."

Kyle looked up. He was in a space with blackboards, faced with little desks with small chairs.

"God, this looks like my second-grade classroom," strangely familiar. He thought of Ms. Noble teaching cursive on the blackboard, and how he would just gaze out the window and daydream.

"Where am I?" he asked, dazed by his surroundings.

"You are in the Land of Letters."

While its voice sounded human, what stepped out of the shadows was far from it.

Standing before him was a being of a rather peculiar shape. It was a letter A, in fact, as odd as that may sound.

"What do you mean?"

"Choose your words carefully, stranger," it warned. "We are not given to waste here."

"Who do you think you're talking to?" Kyle asked angrily.

"There's no need to take that hostile tone," it replied.

Just then another voice piped up. This time, a letter F stepped into the light.

"I wonder if he is a new one. It's been so long, you know, since we've had any new additions."

And yet another revealed himself, a letter D, "Oh my, yes! Wouldn't it be delightful? I've grown awfully sick of seeing the same old faces."

The first creature replied, "Of course not! You two should know better. After all these eons, a new addition is out of the question."

"I am the letter A. Would you care to introduce yourself?"

"I'm Kyle Wilson."

Seeing this mock play and remembering his introduction in the Land of Letters all too well, Kyle was aghast. He yelled, "Stop, Jesus Christ! What the hell is this? You're the craziest bunch of bastards ever! Will anyone tell me how to get out of this hell hole?"

By now Kyle was pacing wildly, but as he did so he could also faintly hear strange voices in the background again…

"Yes, Doctor, he's been thrashing ever since he moved back here," a woman's voice said.

"Nurse, you better call his sister. This could be a sign that he's coming to," a male voice replied.

As the voices faded, WORD came over to Kyle saying, "Calm down, Kyle, really. It's just a few words running around. No need to make such a big fuss. SENTENCE and his colleagues are just trying to get you prepared for your immersion."

"Immersion, just what the hell's that? I'm so damn sick of this place! If I could just get the hell out of here, you'll never have to worry about seeing me again!" Kyle shouted.

"Well, as you can see, it's a part of your life's story that they've rehearsed so well. Now you've just got to orchestrate your own little play," WORD said, very calmly.

"Now what am I supposed to do and to what end?" Kyle asked, calming down as he spoke.

"You can make it whatever you want it to be and for your own purpose," WORD replied.

"Just how do I go about that?" Kyle asked, exasperatedly.

"Come on, let's head up to your so-called Parade Ground," WORD replied.

His head was spinning as he was trying to think of what or how his little show would go, not fully grasping all the nuances of the impending moment.

As they came up to the parade ground, Kyle could see in the background all kinds of letters of the entire alphabet, upper and lower case, lined up, off to the horizon.

MARSHAL came up to the three as they arrived on the field at the Parade Ground. "You three assume your positions," MARSHAL said.

WORD said to Kyle, "By now you know the drill so go ahead, call on the letters as you want them and they'll come on to the field. Remember it's your story, so you get to say it like you want to. THOUGHT and I will watch from the reviewing stand."

Kyle could now hear the strains of *The Stars and Stripes Forever,* and as he dashed on to the field he was calling to letters of the poem he had been composing as they sprang into his mind. He was overcome with a sense of awe as they started streaming across the Parade Ground right in front of him.

WHAT BECOMES

What tho I choose to see and do many, many things,
fear always at the ready, is usually what springs.

Lacking faith and strength to reckon,
I will shrink from opportunities that beckon.

If I choose not to learn the way, these are what befall.
Infant steps are what's required, so as not to fall.

Faith in ourselves comes with years of learning that we can do.
Wisdom follows to know 'we cans' from what we must eschew.

Patience then, if we're to find success, happiness, fulfillment.
Avoiding unsuited things, I deal with those wherein I find agreement.

Achievement of my tasks then follows, as does night the day.
Then God is in his heaven, and faith is belief in my own way.

In sum, with all my different trials, I should've guessed,
all these tribulations have made me self-possessed!

Poof! Everything instantly seemed very different and before he even opened his eyes, Kyle could hear his sister distinctly saying, "Doctor, do you really think he's coming to? Will he be all right? I'm so worried."

Molly took a chair at Kyle's bedside and started chatting. "Hello, Kyle. Are you going to wake up and talk to me? You know you've been asleep now for a long time. Betsy and I have been worried sick about you, and Betsy, well, you better wake up or I'm afraid she's going to write you off."

Just then Kyle opened his eyes. "Oh God, I hope this isn't just another chapter in the most bizarre experience I've ever had!"

"Whatever are you talking about?" Molly said.

"You have no idea, Sis. You might as well say I've been to hell and back!"

PTDD

Later that afternoon, Kyle tried to briefly describe what he had just experienced, relating pretty much the whole story, but his sister, while incredulous on the one hand, became more patronizing as he related his ordeal, saying to him, "Give it time, you've been in a coma for the last few weeks. You'll forget all about it in a day or two."

Kyle, by now too savvy, or maybe too suspicious, saw through all this and flatly told her, "I will like hell! And please stop patronizing me. I know you don't believe a word I said. It was absolute hell!"

Then, feeling badly for having been so abrupt, "Sorry, Sis, I don't mean to be cross. I know you've always been in my corner and I owe you so much. I don't think I could have gotten sober without you."

"Kyle, it's okay. I just hate seeing you get so upset. We all love you and we're just worried about you," Molly said.

He got pretty much the same reaction from Betsy after her overwhelming delight of finally seeing him awake. After smothering Kyle with kisses and hugs and a chorus of, "Oh Kyle, I was so worried about you! I missed you so much! Please don't ever leave me again! You've got to be more careful driving!" She went on, "So tell me how do you feel? Maybe you got that long needed rest. You had been working so hard and all those long hours at the library. I'm sure that's why you were distracted and got into the accident in the first place."

"Oh, for Christ's sake! That doesn't have anything to do with it at all. I barely remember the accident anyway. All I can tell you is that Odysseus has nothing on me! As I was telling Sis before she left, I've been to hell and back! Of course, as usual, she doesn't believe a thing I said. In another sense, I guess I really can't blame her. Who the hell would believe such an outlandish story? I tell you, Betsy, it's beyond words!" Oh, how ironic, he thought, but then catching himself, "Maybe you're right, maybe I did spend too much time at work."

"Any idea how long you'll be here?" Betsy asked.

"Jesus, I just woke up! I have no idea; nobody has said anything to me." Kyle replied.

"I was just hoping you'd be coming home by the end of the week. You remember Julie and Paul were going to get married. Well, the ceremony is this Saturday and I was hoping you'd be able to come!" Betsy said.

"Are you crazy? They're Catholics, aren't they? And I suppose it's going to be at St. Columbus! Anyway, I'm not going anywhere near that damn place. Christ-sake, talk about your immortal soul. Well, if you want to keep it, give that place a wide birth!"

"Kyle, whatever are you talking about? Father Pilate is one of your favorite people," Betsy replied.

"With a name like that, he's no friend of mine! I'll tell you right now you can't trust a one of these religious fanatics. Believe you me, I got it right from Chaucer himself."

"Oh, Kyle, I'm sorry. I guess I was getting ahead of myself. I do want you home again, so badly, but obviously, you need some time to get over all this," Betsy said, totally taken aback and trying to be comforting.

"Get over it! I can't ever imagine getting over this experience! Let me tell you, being held captive by a bunch of letters and words isn't the least bit funny! You'll never understand, but I felt like I was a prisoner in my own mind, if you can believe that! It was unbelievably weird!" Kyle said in an exasperated manner.

Betsy, trying to conceal tears, urged, "Try to get some rest, dear. I'll be back later and please, remember we're going to get through this. Dr. Angle has promised me you're doing well and that you'll be back to your old self soon."

"Dr. Ankle?" Kyle yelled. "I don't want that son of a bitch anywhere near me!"

"Calm down Dear! It's Dr. An-gle."

"Well, regardless of his name, him and that other doctor bear watching. Neither one of them did me any favors."

Just then one of the nurses rushed in, "Is everything alright? It sounded like Mr. Wilson was getting upset."

"Yes, I do think he needs to rest; I was about to go anyway," Betsy replied.

"Betsy, please forgive me. I just don't feel like myself. But really Babe, you have no idea what it's like to have your whole world turned upside down. I just need to get some rest and let things settle a bit."

Betsy joined Molly who was down the hall talking with Dr. Angle.

"I've just been telling the Doctor about Kyle's dream and how mixed up he is," Molly said.

"Oh yes, Doctor," Betsy exclaimed, "he's so mixed up, talking about all these words and letters, saying he talked with Chaucer."

Betsy was crying now.

"He doesn't want anything to do with Father Pilate and says he won't go near the church, let alone attend our friend's wedding this coming Saturday."

"Now, now, dear, there's no need for tears. He'll come around in a day or two. But just to be on the safe side, Dr. Norris, our resident psychiatrist, is going to check in on him. You two should really go home and try to get some rest. Right now, Kyle is confused, a very normal state after such a long period of being unconscious."

Later that day Dr. Norris did stop in to see Kyle. "Hi Kyle, I'm Dr. Norris and I wanted to stop by and see how you're doing. Dr. Angle and your family have expressed some concerns."

"Oh, I'll bet they have! They think I'm making all this stuff up, but I'll tell you it's as real as anything I've ever been through!" Kyle exclaimed.

"Tell me about it; what happened?"

Kyle recounted his recent experiences and his journey in the Land of Letters and the Land of Words and all the adjoining realms.

The Doctor, responding very calmly, "Wow, what an amazing experience! I don't believe I've ever heard anything quite like it! It's a wonder you're not pulling your hair out. I'm pleased to see how well your handling this experience! It must have been awful!"

"You don't know the half of it, Doc, but I'm glad you're at least trying to understand," Kyle said. "Of course, I developed a few misgivings regarding your profession. I've seen firsthand what a mockery you guys can make of just about any situation, not to mention how you and that other doctor abandoned me to my own devices, with my only recourse to just lay back and suck it up."

"Whatever are you talking about?" Dr. Norris asked.

"Doc, I'm not sure how much I can trust you after I saw PSYCHIATRY and PSYCHOLOGY debating some aspects of Life Adjustment Theory. As near as I could make out, everyone was more confused afterwards than before they started," Kyle said.

"How interesting," Dr. Norris commented. "Look, I know you're very distraught over this experience and I'd like to try to help you put this recent experience in perspective. I do think I can help if you're willing."

"Okay, Doc, but no funny business. I don't think I can really deal with any more mind games," Kyle asserted.

"Well, for starters I'd like to run a test or two, and then we can talk some more," the Doctor said.

At the psychiatric staff meeting the next morning, Dr. Norris presented Kyle's case to his colleagues, "Kyle Wilson, a 44-year-old male, is healthy in appearance, and with no physical abnormalities, in spite of some scars on his scalp from a recent auto accident. However, he presents psychiatric manifestations of hostility, abnormal associations and effects from prior auditory and visual hallucinations, while in a dream-like state, induced by traumatic brain injury. Shortly after an auto accident over six weeks ago, he suffered a grand mal seizure, idiopathic in nature, and was subsequently determined to be nearly braindead with a coma-scale response of 7. While in this state, the patient maintains that he was a captive in a mysterious world, initially made up of letters and words of the English language, during the period he was considered to be in a coma. His case is unusual in that there seems to be one rather long, continual narrative addressing social concerns and their relationships to and between letters and words that apparently went on the entire period he was unconscious.

The concern is that the patient is responding to this long event as though it were an actual life experience that he absolutely maintains is of another world. He knows rationally that he was unconscious and in the hospital during this period, but he resolutely believes the events that occurred are real, though he, so far at least, has not been able to give a rational explanation as to where these events took place. Today I'm planning on administering the Word Association Test to see how he compares with the standard non-psychotic profile. Of course, there will also be some talk therapy to get a general impression if it appears at all likely that he might be amenable to some form of cognitive therapy. I'll update the group at tomorrow's staff meeting."

On Kyle's floor the nurse came into his room, "And how are we doing this morning? I'm Bernese. Dr. Angle asked me to keep an eye on you," she announced.

"Look, I don't want to hear the mention of any eye in my room. I've had an eye looking over my shoulder for the last six weeks so give me a break, will you? As it is, I had to sleep with one eye open worrying the *Eye of Providence* would show up again."

"Oh, I'm so sorry!" Bernese said. "Why don't you just relax. I know it's tough being in bed and I'm sure your first night was difficult. It's just about this time you woke up yesterday."

Kyle could hear the radio playing from his roommate's side of the room, "It's radio station W-O-R-D from Salem, the station where the word is music. Good morning to our listeners out there. We're continuing with our week, celebrating Franz Joseph Hayden. If you were listening yesterday, I hope you enjoyed his *Surprise Symphony*."

Kyle, speaking over the radio, "Yeah, I just loved it! I wish you could have seen the play that was going on where I was. Well, you can't get me now WORD; I'm finally on the other side."

The announcer continued, "Well, this morning I'm going to play Hayden's, Symphony No. 47, sometimes referred to as the *Palindrome Symphony*, for obvious reasons that I'm sure our devoted listeners are aware of."

"Jesus Christ, are you kidding me!" Kyle exclaimed, then half-chuckled.

The nurse turned to him, saying, "Are you all right?"

"Oh yeah, it's nothing. Palindromes for me now, yeah I get it, *able was I ere I saw Elba*, another damn word game! Where does it end? Oh, no, it's nothing at all!" he said sarcastically.

"I'll ask your roommate, Mr. Noteworthy, to turn his radio down. Sometimes he just keeps it blaring. Yesterday his morning music was so beautiful and then all of a sudden it started blaring, *The Stars and Stripes Forever*, and I had to ask him to turn it down then too," the nurse said.

"Yeah, now that was the one thing that really was music to my ears," Kyle remarked.

Just then Dr. Norris entered saying, "How you doing this morning, Kyle?"

"I'm tryin', Doc. What's up?"

"Thought I'd stop by and see how you're feeling. Maybe we could talk a little bit. I also have a test that I think might be helpful."

"Okay Doc, but I hardly slept last night," Kyle replied.

"Really, now why do you suppose that was?"

"Jesus, Doc, guess I'm scared as hell I won't wake up again."

"You can't worry about that, Kyle. You have to learn to cope with this experience. Please try to remember that no actual harm came to you."

"Yeah, easy for you to say. How would you like being caught in a world where everything is baffling and nothing appears to be what it really is?" Kyle peered questioningly at the doctor.

"I know it's difficult, but try to keep the faith," he advised in turn.

"Oh, that's a good one, Doc. Keep the faith, huh? Any faith I had went out the window about six weeks ago."

"Easy does it, Kyle. Don't be so hard on yourself. All any of us have is '*now*' and I'm here and nothing's going to happen to you right now. So, try to relax for a bit and let's just start with this little test. If nothing else, it will get you involved."

"You're the boss, Doc."

"Good. I'm going to say a word and I'd like you to respond to it with the first word or phrase that comes to your mind. Okay?"

"Yeah, sure Doc."

"The first word is Beauty."
"Monocle," Kyle replied.

"Alone."
"One."

"Life."
"Death."

"Red."
"Art."

"Stove."
"Oven."

"Cardboard."
"Box."

"Bicycle."
"Wheel."

"Food."
"Dinner."

"Animal."
"Dog."

"Person."
"Mirror."

"Car."
"Driver."

"Music."
"Opera."

"Unique."
"Prism."

"Word."
"Emoji."

"Very good, that will do."

"So, what's the verdict Doc, am I crazy?"

"No, no, but some of your responses do make me curious. Perhaps we could talk about a few of them if you feel up to it?"

"Yeah, sure, Doc. What d' you want to know?"

"Well then, let me ask you, I say 'alone' and you say 'one'. What's up with that?"

"It's good you're sitting, Doc. So, hang on to your seat. Look, I hadn't been in the Land of Words but a little bit before the word ALONE is up giving a speech and, believe me, his looks, well he was a dead-ringer for the cardinal number, one, and, to top it off, he starts out saying that he couldn't ever remember being more himself than the time he was beside himself with worry, then adding, if you can picture a number eleven standing beside a crumpled ball of paper that never looked the same twice, the ball of paper being the word WORRY, of course!"

"Wow, very interesting. How did that seem to you and what was your reaction?"

"Jesus, Doc, what do you think? I already knew the place was crazy, but you know, 'when in Rome'! Anyway, I just decided to suck it up! Course I might have put my foot down right there if I had only known what was coming."

"I guess I don't understand why this was so terrifying. I mean, sure it's odd and all that, but it doesn't seem that terrifying to me," the Doctor said.

"Look, Doc, I've spent my last few years managing books, writing proposals, and drafting reports, turning words this way and that, and then to have these upstart letters and words running around like people, making judgments and all, well, it was more than I could take. What's more, I found myself explaining to these creatures about my difficulties learning to spell and my early childhood anxiety."

"That's incredible, Kyle. I'm amazed you're so forthcoming with such intimate details."

"Jesus, Doc, I didn't have much choice. The setting was so weird that this stuff just tumbled out as situations arose. At first the letters showed me combinations of letters that were really haunting, like *'childhood anxiety'*, and then they had me joining in word games. In the first game, I headed up the phrase, 'I'm my own man.' Next thing I knew they come up with the rejoinder, 'who is self-possessed.' Then it was off to a crossword, where I led the phrase 'I am who I am.' This, of course, led to the Land of Words where things really went crazy."

"Looking back, I'm just amazed to recognize the role that spelling and grammar have played in my life. And even as an adult I continually find myself looking up spelling for words, as well as often searching my books and the web to make sure a phrase is correct, not to mention seeing puns everywhere. I guess my early struggles with these basics is really a metaphor for my difficult development."

"Yes, Kyle, I guess that's why they call childhood the formative years?"

"What about your response to the word 'person'? You said 'mirror' and I just wonder what would make you say that."

"Let me tell you, Doc, that was one of the scariest moments. There's the word PERSON, looking like a large vanity mirror and, of course, there I was, a small vanity mirror, right smack in the middle of him, looking down at myself embodying him! That scared the living bejesus out of me."

"I guess I have a hard time understanding why you personally felt so threatened. No one tried to hurt you. It seems to me your journey was really one of exposure to new viewpoints and ideas. You do know the old saying, 'life is an education'?"

"Yeah, sure, Doc, anything you say. Of course, all the time I could hear all you guys in the hospital writing me off just like I was an old plug being sent off to the glue factory. All the while the words were working me. At one point, they even got me to drink again. Next thing I knew, I turned into a reprobate and that wasn't very pretty, let me tell you. The two things I've learned are that you better cover your ass, and that you keep one eye over your shoulder; that's all I know."

"Just a couple more of these words," the Doctor said. "What about unique? Why did 'prism' come to mind?"

"Doc, that was really amazing! This thing that looks just like a prism introduces himself as the word UNIQUE and then he launches into this poem called, *I Am.* That really got me to thinkin' about personal identity. I mean, what the hell, who ever really knows who they are, why they're here, what's it all about and that sort of thing. Sure as hell got me to thinkin'."

"What was the upshot of it then?" the Doctor asked.

"Hell, in the final analysis, he didn't know either and I give him credit for that. It was like in the end he throws up his hands and says, 'I don't have the answer, so I'm just going to get on and enjoy the life I have;' in my mind an honest being," Kyle said.

"Very interesting, very interesting. What about you, Kyle? Do you buy that point, of getting on with life?" the Doctor asked.

"I don't know, Doc. It's all so weird and so fresh in my mind. I'm just not ready to put it down yet."

"In time, Kyle, in time. Tell me, Kyle, what about the word that you responded to with the word emoji? What's going on there?"

"Oh no, Doc. You got it wrong. Not just any word. It was the word, WORD, and, I have to add, a spitting image of the *Face with Tears of Joy* emoji. Of course, that isn't all. Next thing I find out is he's married to ETYMOLOGY, if you can believe that."

"Really, Kyle, isn't that a bit illogical; English is gender neutral, you know."

"Oh, Doc, I know it sounds unbelievable, but he had all the answers. He had me at his home where I met his wife too, but when I asked about this gender business that you mention, he told me to look at our own English-speaking world. Then he asked me if I knew who's doing what with whom? He said it seems like anything goes in our world, gender be damned, adding that it's no different in the Land of Words, that the apple doesn't fall very far from the tree, laying the blame squarely at the feet of the humankind. He went on to say there are some unlikely matchups in their world, but they remain pretty much under wraps, or as we would say, in the closet. Apparently, privacy is something that they respect in the Land of Words."

"Surely you know that etymology and the history of words are far more complex than you suggest. Words are derived from other words, from other languages, or arise out of new technology. It's really a whole discipline called philology."

"Look, Doc, technically, I know that's supposed to be the case, but I was right in their home, where WORD and ETYMOLOGY had a nursery that was full of new words just starting out. Now, come to find out I see he got top billing last year from the *Oxford Dictionaries* who named this emoji Word of The Year!" Kyle replied.

"Come now, Kyle, you don't really think there's any link, do you?" the Doctor asked, with raised eyebrow.

"Oh no, Doc, course not! It's only a coincidence, just like this damn radio station, W-O-R-D isn't, not to mention the Palindrome Symphony and one of the nurses keeping an 'eye' on me. No, no, nothing to it at all Doc!" Kyle said, sarcasm dripping from his voice.

"Kyle, really, take it easy. No one's out to get you. Everyone here is trying to help and Bernese, well she's the best. I'm sure there was nothing sinister in her saying that. You know it's a common figure of speech."

"Forgive me, Doc. I'm really on edge this morning. Not sleeping much last night didn't help either."

"That's okay, Kyle. Don't worry about it, I'm going to have Bernese give you a little something to help you relax. Okay? And please remember we're here to help. Call if you need anything and I'll be back later today to look in. I hear your lady friend, Betsy, and your sister will be dropping by. You're lucky to have a family that's so supportive."

"Thanks, Doc."

Later in the afternoon Betsy did come by. "How you doing Honey?"

"Better, Babe. The Doc gave me a little something that really helped me get some rest. God, I was feeling awful this morning and weird too."

"Oh, I'm so glad to hear that. As soon as you get out of here we're going to take some time off, maybe even a trip to Italy to see some of the museums you've always talked about."

"I don't know, Babe, it's a little early for that. Not sure I'm quite ready for so much, and art, well I need a little time before I'm ready to deal with that."

"What's going on, Honey, you know how you love art."

"I know, but I just had a couple of brushes with art that I'm still trying to figure out. You want to talk about lively colors, you don't know the half of it. Then there was this big primary color – Red – boy he didn't fool around. I have to say he knew how to moderate an audience, but it surely was very unnerving, the way they knew I was there and all. They actually called on me and had me at the podium speaking at this large conference."

"Kyle, let it go. You're just getting yourself all worked up."

Just then Molly entered the room, "How're you doing, Kyle? You look so much better."

"Hi, Sis. Yeah, I'm feeling better."

After chatting for a bit, the two women left and once out of the room they agreed to stop and see Dr. Norris. After greeting, Betsy asked, "What do you think, Doctor, how's he doing?"

"I think he's doing quite well, all things considered. It's very apparent he's had quite a trauma! So naturally, he's expressing a fair amount of hostility and a good degree of anxiety. I did prescribe a sedative this morning that helped him get some rest and the nurse says he appears to be more relaxed," the doctor said.

"We both thought he seemed much better than he was yesterday," Molly said.

"Yes, I do think he's improving. Talking with him this morning seemed to ease his mind, and he was quite able to express himself, although he continues to indulge this fantasy life while he was in the coma. Tell me, Molly, is there anything else you can add about his childhood?"

"Oh, Doctor, he was such a cute little boy! But, oh, how very precocious he was! Although early on he had real problems getting along with other children, he always had a funny way with words and language. And, as I've already mentioned, he was finally taken to a therapist, where he was diagnosed with that condition, I think you call it, Social Communication Disorder."

"Oh, yes, that certainly fits. And I think you said before that it helped," the Doctor replied.

"Oh, definitely, Doctor, he seemed to adjust quite well after just a few months. Doctor, he's grown up to be such a wonderful man. Now he's a supervisor at the library where he works. Of course, he had a tough run, as I've already told you, what with the family problems and his turn to alcohol. I just think it's amazing how he turned his life around," Molly said.

"Well, this is very useful information. I'm sure this recent episode will pass, and it shouldn't be too long before Kyle is back to himself. So if you ladies will excuse me, I'm about to stop down to see him," the Doctor said.

After the women left, Doctor Norris went to see his patient, "How you doing, Kyle?"

"Okay, Doc. Betsy and my sister stopped by a little while ago. It was good to see them."

"Yes, they stopped by to see me too, and they are obviously happy to see that you're feeling better."

"Yeah, Doc, but they're still patronizing me."

"What do you expect? You have to expect some raised eyebrows with these stories you tell. You do know that, right?"

"I know, Doc. Jesus, what am I supposed to do? I'm only recounting what I experienced. You're not suggesting I pretend it didn't happen, are you?"

"No, no, nothing of the sort, but why even go there with them, or, for that matter, with most other people? Anything you have got to say about your experience you can share with me. That's what I'm here for. We'll figure this thing out together."

"What's to figure out, Doc? I told you what happened, so what the hell can you do about it, that's what I'd like to know."

"Kyle, I mean we'll try to understand this experience together. If nothing else, I think as you look back on it more carefully with me, that you may see this experience in a different light."

"And you think that will help, Doc? I'd sure as hell like to know how!"

"Definitely, understanding it will make it seem a lot less mysterious and creepy."

"You're the Doctor, but I sure do wonder how this will help."

"So look, Kyle, I'll be back tomorrow morning and we'll continue talking about these things, but before I go, tell me a little bit about this business where you were involved with a 'burning bush'."

"Oh, God! But I do mean GOD the word. Yes, this was very mysterious. That bush, he said he was the word GOD, but in that room, everyone deferred to him like he was God and how the hell are you supposed to know who God is or what he or she looks like anyway? Of course, the thing I couldn't get over was when he told this story, *Close to Heaven*. This story pretty much dismissed any of the common notions or ideas that people have of God. In fact, the whole episode with him was very unusual for that reason. He didn't proselytize or pitch any particular view about religion. Oh, all the other ones in the room took one position or another, but not GOD! He kind of left it open, as though you had to search your own soul or make your own judgments regarding the existence of a supreme being! I have to admit I'm still totally confused," Kyle said.

"There's no shame in being confused. I'd be worried if you weren't. After all, it isn't every day you meet God or shall we say his namesake!"

"That sure makes me feel a little better, Doc. I'm glad I'm not the only one who sees this as pretty amazing! Glad you're on my side."

"Well, this all is certainly very interesting. Definitely, food for thought, as they say. I'm going to run along for now, but I'll see you tomorrow."

"Take care, Doc."

At the staff meeting the next morning, Dr. Norris updated Kyle's case with his colleagues:

"After a long session with the patient, Kyle Wilson, and also having spoken with his family, some aspects of the case seem quite apparent. First, let me say that as a young man the patient was diagnosed with Social (Pragmatic) Communication Disorder. His sister related that he was a very precocious child with an extraordinary sense and use of words. With therapy he seemed to adjust to his social environment, but later on in life, due to early childhood and family problems, he turned to alcohol, was hospitalized for a serious suicide episode, was diagnosed with suicidal ideation and with adult adjustment disorder. After a number of years in therapy and finally through a 12-step program, to deal with his addiction, he largely resolved his inner conflicts and went on to be quite proficient in his profession as a librarian."

"His recent experience of a long continued narrative journey with letters and words while in a dream-like state appears to have gone on during the entire period the patient was in a coma. Upon regaining consciousness, the patient is easily agitated by situations that remind him of his recent experience, and he can become hostile and quite assertive when patronized by staff or family. The case is remarkable for the consistency and apparent authenticity that the patient expresses when relating any aspect of the experience. There is a definite post-traumatic element to his experience as he continues to be anxious about falling asleep and or being caught up in his imaginary world. While conscious, he also continues to experience and react to some objective situations and things as though they are connected to this other world."

"Concurrent to his associations with letters and words, as well as being privy to professional discussions of his case while in an unconscious state, there was a profound recapitulation of traumatic events in his life with a resulting degree of dream-work that is unique in my experience and without any comparable narratives in the literature. There is also a comparable development throughout this experience that equates his early difficulties with spelling and grammar to his ongoing struggle for growth and maturity, something he now feels quite sure about."

"I have also been unable to find any listed psychiatric disorder with a similar psychopathology in the literature. Undoubtedly, there are cases of nightmares with patients expressing fear of falling asleep, but those nightmares, which can be recurrent, are usually of a short duration and usually revolve around one situation or dimension of personality and usually are not manifest in any conscious behavior. Of course, there are numerous cases of Post Traumatic Stress Disorder where patients have recurrent nightmares in response to a repressed prior experience. However, I could find no similar case or established psychiatric disorder that applies in this case. I am therefore recommending to the staff that this case be fully written up and submitted as a journal article. The thrust of the article will be the establishment of a newly identified condition called, **Post Traumatic Dream Disorder** (PTDD)."

There was some clapping by the staff at this conclusion and the chief psychiatrist said, "Excellent presentation, Doctor. I'd like very much to meet this young man."

Later that morning both doctors went to Kyle's room and Dr. Norris introduced the chief.

"Kyle, I'd like you to meet our chief psychiatrist, Dr. Brainard. He's very interested in your situation and really wanted to meet you."

"Hi Kyle, Dr. Norris has explained what happened to you, and it appears it's a rather remarkable story. He's planning on writing all this up for a journal article, as this is a very unusual case. He's going to make a celebrity out of you. How do you feel about that?"

"Look, Doc, after the characters that I've been associating with, nothing will surprise me. I've already told Doctor Norris about my burning-bush experience, so I think anything you guys do will have to go quite a way to top that!"

"Really, I'm curious. Care to tell me about it?" Dr. Brainard probed.

"Yeah, it is pretty amazing, I guess," Kyle said. "I got into this book, *Words in Modern Interpretations of the Biblical Literature*, where I then went on to the *Tower of Babel* and it was quite an experience. That's where I met him, the word GOD, that is, or, as Dr. Norris put it so well, 'God's namesake.' I still don't know what to make of it all. And I know that you guys don't really believe this happened; you think this is something I imagined or conjured up and you're just interested because you're trying to understand why, but you gotta admit, Doc, it's one hell of a story!"

"That's true," the Doctor replied. "Yes, we're trying to understand what happened, and it is one hell of a story too, but we do look at it a little differently than you do. Can we all agree though, between us here, it's something we're all trying to understand and that hopefully you'll feel a lot more comfortable about it as you look back over those events with Dr. Norris in the next few days?"

"Whatever you say, Doc, but remember at the end of the day, you'll never exactly be able to climb into my shoes or retrace my steps."

"We have no intention of trying to do that, but maybe walking back through a little of this with us at your side just might change your views a little bit. After all, what have you got to lose? You've got three squares and a cot here, with waitresses no less. So give us a little time and we'll see where things are in a few days," Doctor Brainard said.

"When you put it that way, Doc, how can I say no?" Kyle retorted.

"Good, then Dr. Norris will continue to follow up with you."

Over the next few days, Dr. Norris and Kyle met several times, discussing the period while he was in the coma, including, of course, his memories of the events and how and why he reacted the way he did.

It was Friday morning when Dr. Norris came to see his patient. "How you feeling this morning, Kyle? I think this is the day for you to get back to your family."

"Really, Doc? I guess I'm as ready as I'll ever be. You know I never thought I'd be able to put all this behind me. It really helped trying to understand it all. Maybe one of these days I'll write a book or something."

"You've done really well, Kyle. I think you now have put this experience in the proper perspective, and in a very special way I think it was a great experience for you. It would appear that this episode was in great measure an intense period of therapy, in a manner of speaking. Once you reflected on it all, I think you've really managed to settle and give closure to a lot of the issues in your life," the Doctor said.

"Yeah, not everybody has the dubious distinction of being responsible for the creation of a newly minted psychiatric condition like PTDD or a place in the psychiatric literature. And how many can say they literally got the 'word' directly from GOD's namesake and got off as easily as I did!" Kyle asserted his point. This time, with a smile.

***